The Demise of
Alexis Vancamp

The Demise of Alexis Vancamp

Karen Williams

URBAN BOOKS

www.urbanbooks.net

Urban Books, LLC
300 Farmingdale Road, NY-Route 109
Farmingdale, NY 11735

The Demise of Alexis Vancamp
Copyright © 2013 Karen Williams

ISBN 13: 978-1-60162-131-3
ISBN 10: 1-60162-131-0

First Mass Market Printing May 2019
First Trade Paperback Printing May 2013
Printed in the United States of America

10 9 8 7 6 5 4 3 2 1

*This is a work of fiction. Any references or similar-
ities to actual events, real people, living or dead,
or to real locales are intended to give the novel a
sense of reality. Any similarity in other names,
characters, places, and incidents is entirely coin-
cidental.*

Distributed by Kensington Publishing Corp.
Submit Orders to:
Customer Service
400 Hahn Road
Westminster, MD 21157-4627
Phone: 1-800-733-3000
Fax: 1-800-659-2436

This novel is dedicated to my fans. Without you guys I'm nothing. Your support means a lot to me . . . Thank You.

Acknowledgments

Thanks for checking in with me again. I feel positively elated as I write these acknowledgments . . . My heart is filled with nothing but joy right now. This year I was blessed to have one of my dreams come into fruition. I became a home buyer. For me this is such a big freaking deal. I now have a foundation for my kids and family. To come where I come from and have the struggles I've had and accomplish this? It's surreal to me. One thing I always tell the minors I work with is that in the midst of the chaos and the struggles that we often deal with alone, we are afraid to dream because those dreams in the context of how hard life is seem too big and no longer probable. The one thing I always tell them is we can still dream big and do big, despite the struggles, despite the losses. I am forever living proof of this.

To my kids: I love you Adara and Bralynn! Adara thank you so much for keeping an eye on Bralynn so I could focus. You two mean the world to me. I have the best kids! Thank you big sister Crystal and mom for always supporting me. I look up to you so much Crystal and you're making major moves. Mom, thank you so much for always being there for me. I love you! Mikayla and Madyeson I love you two. Yes, I am a rough around the edges auntie, but I love you guys and I have your back always, trust! Donnie I'm proud of you. Hey to Mu-Mu, Jabrez, and Devin. Thank You Trudy for the love you show to my family!

Thanks to my friends Sheryl, Lenzie, Christina, Kimberly, Linda, Tracy, Christina, Talamontes, Pam, Carla, Sewiaa, Ronisha RIP, Tina, Shumeka, Valerie Hoyt, Tara, Pearlean, Maxine, Dena, Barbara, Henrietta, Candis, VI, Phillipo, Latonya, Leigh and Lili, Yvonne Gainer, Monica Burton, Sandra V, Sandra T, Ivy, Clarissa, Daphne and Lydia, Mrs. Pope, Robert, Tiffany, Aparichio. We'll miss you Jose! Eddie Chisym, you always gave me words of encouragement. From the day I met you, you believed in me more than I believed in myself. I needed that at a time where I lost myself and didn't know my own strength or abilities anymore. I do now. I'm stronger than I ever knew, with plenty of gifts to share.

Chris Morales. You don't know what type of impact you have. I've said this before, I know I am a better person for knowing you. I have never met anyone like you before. Your commitment to change the lives of the minors we work with is admirable beyond means. You don't always get the credit you deserve for all you do and you do it all with such a humble spirit. God bless you.

Thank you to all the Book Clubs that supported me. Thanks to Shawnda Hamilton and Papaya Flagstaff. Thank You Radiah. Hey, Netta!

Chucking the peace sign to my author friends: Mondell Pope, Aleta Williams, Terra Little, Terry Wroten, Angel Williams, Rainne Grant and Ahem (Clearing my throat) Author DeTerrius Woods. I'm so proud of you! That's my boo right there! Loreal Ballou, you're up!

Thank You Carl and Natalie Weber.

Kevin Dwyer, we are back at it again. I'm biting my nails waiting for your edits . . . Lol. Seriously, you are the absolute best and I'm so happy you are on this project with me.

And once again, I want to thank my fans. You guys make me feel so honored, as an author. I promise you guys I am going to get over this fear of flying and do more traveling so I can meet you all face to face!

I hope I didn't miss anyone. I'm so sorry if I did. Let me know and I will get you in the next book.

Acknowledgments

Now about the book! Penning it gave me nothing but chills. I don't want to give anything away before you get a chance to read, but prepare to get mind humped!

Until next time . . . Kisses!

Prologue

I couldn't stop myself from sobbing as the police asked me to give an account of what happened. Every time I attempted to explain what unfolded in my living room, I would break down again due to the trauma. The male police officer stared at me impatiently. I wiped my face and my runny nose. "I'm trying my best, Officer. I'm so sorry."

He huffed out an impatient breath.

His partner, a petite white female, gave me a gentle look. "Sweetie. Take a deep breath."

I did as she said, inhaling deeply.

"Now let it out slowly."

I complied.

"Continue that as long as you need to so you calm down, because you certainly can't tell us what happened being upset the way you are. There is a dead body in the room so we know that has to be hard for you. You let us know when you're ready."

I nodded and continued to do as she said. A couple minutes later, when I felt my body return to a slightly normal state, I took another breath and let it out. "Okay. I think I'm ready."

Both officers opened their pads and held their pens in anticipation of my words. I swallowed hard and began recounting the story.

He was going down on me. My legs were wrapped around his neck. And I was so into the feelings it gave me that I almost didn't see Dannon standing in the doorway with flowers in his arms and a mortified expression on his face. In fact, I only acknowledged his presence well after I climaxed. I then shoved Santana's naked body away.

"Dannon!" I said in surprise.

The flowers fell from his arms. Santana looked Dannon's way, with a smirk on his face.

"How long has this shit been going on?" he demanded of me. My normally calm fiancé who rarely cursed was yelling.

Santana, unconcerned with the conversation, sat on the couch next to me as I tried to cover up.

"Not long," I stammered.

Tears ran down Dannon's face. "You do realize that in three weeks we are supposed to get married?"

I looked away and pulled on my dress. "I'm so sorry, Dannon. I didn't mean to hurt you or expose—"

"Expose the fact that you been fucking around on me? After all we have been through together. How could you, selfish bitch?"

Santana threw his head back and cackled. I gave him a sharp look, which he simply ignored. At this point, Dannon was sobbing. I felt so bad that I had brought this hurt to him.

"I guess there is nothing left to say, is it, Alexis? This . . . It speaks for itself . . ." Each word sounded so choppy because he paused between each one with a sob.

I didn't know what to say to that. I had loved Dannon for as long as I could remember. He was my high school sweetheart, my prom date, my first . . . And he was supposed to be my husband. We were supposed to live a perfect life together. I knew better than what I was doing. I was about to lose what I had dreamed about having for years: Dannon as my husband. And, yet, the thought of Santana between my legs again and the anticipation of his thick penis in my walls seemed to make up for not having any of that. I realized that I didn't want that life anymore. The only thing I wanted was Santana. And letting the chips fall where they may was the way to get that. I was more relieved that Dannon had discovered this. And that meant more to me than his tears. He would just have to get over it. He would.

"I knew something was going on. For the past month, you have not been the same. But I kept ignoring all the obvious signs. I have avoided this for as long as I could. It's over."

Yes. Before I could respond, he walked out of my apartment.

I felt a sense of elation that I was now able to be with Santana freely and not sneak around. I also no longer had to divide my time between him and Dannon. I was now all his.

"Thank fucking God that emotional-ass nigga gone!" Santana yelled.

He leaned over my legs, split them apart, slipped between them, and slid inside of me. At the feel of his big dick, my sadness was replaced with lust as he pounded into me. I was so into it that I almost didn't see Dannon come back into my apartment. I tried to shove Santana away but he refused to get off of me and continued to fuck me.

With wide eyes I watched as Dannon slipped off his engagement ring and set it on my coffee table. Normally men didn't wear an engagement ring. Dannon was different from the *average man. The day he had proposed to me, he put one on his finger as well and said from that day forward he was going to live the life of a married man. Tears were running down his face and still all I could think about was how good Santana felt being inside of me. What had this man done to me?*

Dannon walked out again.

Santana squeezed one of my nipples roughly.

I moaned and jumped when I saw Dannon standing in front of us yet again!

Dannon pulled a gun out of his back pocket, aimed it toward his chest, and fired several times. I screamed as he fell to the floor and blood oozed out of his chest.

Dannon had killed himself.

"And that's what happened."

I opened my eyes again to find both officers looking at me. Disgust was in their eyes. They weren't in my world, so I cared very little about their perception of me. I didn't want Dannon to die but I also didn't pull the trigger. It was idiotic for anyone to blame me for this. But, still, seeing someone take their life in front of you was definitely a frightening thing. . . .

The woman said, "So after he fired those shots, he fell down and he never got back up again?"

"Yes. He didn't move after that."

They both scribbled this down.

Another officer came back into the house. He was the one who escorted Santana outside and left him there. Once they stopped talking, the female officer said, "You two are in the clear. Thank you for your time."

Chapter 1

A Month Before

When everything was oh so perfect in my life and couldn't get any better, Santana walked in. I was the proud daughter of successful parents. My dad owned property all around southern California, as well as a tow truck business. My mother was a social worker and I had graduated at the top of my class at UCLA, in business and accounting. I worked for my father as a property supervisor. I was over all my daddy's property managers; I dealt with all the finances. His company was called Vancamp Equities, Inc. It was located in Lakewood, California, on Candlewood Street. I also did the HR work: hiring and firing, paychecks. All of it.

He didn't have to worry about a thing. My sister had just started college at Spelman. She, being a little wilder than I was, wanted to branch off on her own. I was engaged to one of the greatest guys on the planet, Dannon. I sighed thinking about him. He was my high school sweetheart and was three years older than I. Both his parents, who loved me, were doctors, and Dannon was working on his residency at Harbor-UCLA Medical Center. He was every bit of handsome. He was six foot three with creamy dark brown skin, and had a set of pearly whites. I was his queen and that's how he treated me. He said he couldn't live without me. I believed him. We had been together for over ten years, since I was fourteen.

The day Santana walked into my work office, I was busy getting time cards done so I could go home and get ready for a date night with my man. My dad had called me at the last minute, and told me he had a young gentleman for me to interview for on-site maintenance work at our Paramount complex. Santana was just what he felt he needed. I told my daddy okay, but I really didn't have time for an interview. I wanted to go home, and take my time bathing and getting pretty for Dannon. With his residency he was always so busy, so he had been lucky enough to get a Friday night off. Dannon wanted the night to be special. He was going to take me to his favorite restaurant: Ruth's Chris Steak House, in Anaheim. I wanted to take full advantage of our night together.

Glancing at my watch, I saw the interviewee was thirty minutes late. "I love you, baby," I cooed into the phone to Dannon as I reviewed a time card.

"Same here. I can't wait to see you tonight and make love to you."

I purred into the phone, "You want me to wear something special for you?"

"You know I do." He started telling me how his day was. I listened intently.

I signed off on a time card and looked at my watch again. Forty-five minutes had passed. It would just be his loss. There was no way I would ever hire someone who was that damn late for an interview.

"Okay, baby. Let me get off this phone so I can go home and get dressed."

"See you later, babe."

I made a kiss sound into the phone before hanging up. I then stood, put on my jacket, and grabbed my purse and briefcase. That's when I heard a knock at the door.

Agitated, I turned and looked at who my visitor was. *No, he didn't have the nerve to show up this late.*

I arrogantly studied him as he walked into the room. He was handsome nonetheless. He had brown skin and jet-black curly hair, telling me he was mixed. I figured he had to be Spanish and black. He wasn't as tall as Dannon. He seemed to be six feet but he was muscular. It wasn't hard to see that because the fool was wearing a wife beater tucked into a pair of slacks. *Who wears a wife beater to an interview?*

"How you doing, ma'am? I'm Santana Marcelino." He held his hand out for me to shake. I looked at it disdainfully. Not only was he late, he was not dressed properly for an interview and his fingernails were filthy.

I shook my head at him. He was old enough to know better. "You are fifty minutes late. I'm on my way out."

"I'm sorry. I have been having car problems. It stopped twice on the way here and I had to get a jump."

That is the number one excuse for being late to an interview.

"Just give me a chance please," he pleaded. "I really need a job."

I rolled my eyes, and sat down. *At least he can't go to the labor board and say I didn't give him a chance.*

But I knew, even before he answered the routine questions, I wasn't going to hire his ass. I only hired the best employees for my father. And to me, his tacky ass just wasn't that. I knew we needed some of our managers to be a little rough around the edges, like Larry, at our Compton complex, but with how competitive the market was now in terms of employment, I knew I could find much better. Someone who could reflect our company's professionalism.

He stared at me anxiously, clasping his hands between his knees.

I didn't bother asking for a resume. Hell, he didn't have on a shirt! "Do you have any experience performing maintenance work for a forty-unit complex?"

"No. But I'm a fast learner. I know how to fix stuff and—"

I didn't want to hear that line so I cut him off. "What is your highest level of education?"

"Tenth grade. But—"

"Do you have any convictions? DUIs?"

He paused, then said, "Yes. But I can explain them."

I knew all I needed to know. Screw a formal interview with him. He was wasting my time. "Okay. Thank you for your time. You will hear something back from us within two to five business days." I stood and stiffly held out my hand.

He remained seated and looked at me like I was crazy. "Wait. That's it? That's all you want to know?"

"Yes. Like I said, you will hear something back in two to five business days."

His lips snarled and he looked at me angrily. "Fuck that 'two to five business days' line. Are you going to give me a chance or not?" he demanded.

Who does he think he is? "Sir—"

"Are you going to hire me or not?"

"No. You came to the interview late, not properly dressed, and with no res—"

Before I could finish he took one of his arms and knocked everything on my desk to the floor. I gasped and took a step back.

"You fucking bitch."

My heart started pounding fast. I placed a hand on my chest.

As he stormed out of my office, a text message came through on my phone. I ignored it, fearful that he would come back. But he didn't. I got up, locked my door, and went to retrieve my phone.

I took a deep breath as my heart rate slowed down. The text was from Dannon:

> Alexis, I have some bad news. I can't get off tonight. I love you but I gotta go. Make it up to you, sweets.

"Damn," I muttered. *First I get cursed out by a thug and now my baby cancels.* Well, who cared about the thug? I'd never have to see him again. He legitimized everything I felt about him based on how he just acted. But I was disappointed with not being able to see my man tonight.

I might as well get some work done. I turned on my iPod and put one of my playlists that included Eric Roberson, Beyoncé, Dwele, Anthony David, Tank, Raheem DeVaughn, Jazmine Sullivan; and I got to work. I would be so happy when my baby was done with his residency. I knew being a doctor was going to be hectic for us, but once we married and he paid his dues it would change. Realistically I knew he would always be busy, but once we were married we would be living together. So, off the bat, that was more time.

I left my office pretty late. But since my office was located in a typically quiet and safe area I wasn't concerned. I set my attaché case on the concrete near my car so I could dig in my Gucci clutch bag for my keys.

It was hard to locate my keys because I had so much stuff in there. I sighed and pulled my wallet, phone, and my makeup bag out. I held all that stuff in one hand, and searched in my purse with the other. When I felt the cold iron of the keys against my fingers, I grabbed them. But before I could press the alarm to unlock the door, someone slapped me so hard I lost my balance and fell onto the concrete. I stared at the figure that hovered over me and screamed. He was wearing a ski mask.

That's when a gun was pressed in my face. "Shut the fuck up."

My right cheek burned. I closed my eyes at the burning and to block out the sight of the gun. My heart started beating so fast. I was scared shitless. Was he going to rob me? Rape me? Kill me? Or all three? I knew I needed to cooperate with him.

"First off, you dumb ho, push all that shit toward me."

Since I had dropped everything in my hand when I was slapped, everything was on the ground near me. I scooted it all toward him.

He leaned over and picked everything up, saying, "Don't look at me!"

I kept my eyes down.

"Off with that ring, too!"

At my millisecond of hesitation, his gun made a clicking sound. I jumped and shrieked when it did. He leaned down, gripped my hair, and shoved the gun in my face again. "Shut the fuck up before I kill you, tramp."

I nodded. He gripped my left hand and forced my engagement ring off my finger. He tucked it in his pocket along with my wallet and phone. Then he used the keys to open my Infiniti.

"Get in the back seat."

I started crying again, not knowing what was next for me. "Please don't hurt me."

When I guess I didn't move fast enough for him, he gripped my hair and shoved me into the back seat of the car. I landed on my back. He immediately straddled me and slid between my legs. "Sorry, bitch. I need this car and I don't ever leave witnesses."

He was going to kill me! I panicked and tried to fight him and beg him at the same time. "No! Please!"

He smacked me, making my head reel backward. He aimed the gun at me. I prayed silently. Before he got a chance to pull the trigger, he was snatched up by someone. I sat up in the car and watched a man wrap his arm around his neck. When he moved his head back to avoid being head-butted, I saw it was Santana.

He gripped dude's hand that held the gun until the man screamed. Santana punched him repeatedly in his face with his free hand, until he slumped against him, breathing heavily.

"Get the fuck off me, nigga!" Santana slammed him on the concrete. The man scurried to his feet as Santana grabbed the gun off the ground. He pointed it at the dude.

"Give her, her shit back!"

Dude hurried up and pulled my items out of his pocket and handed them back to me.

He backed up some and Santana said, "Now get the fuck out of here!"

The guy started running for his life.

Chapter 2

I held my hand to my chest and breathed a sigh of relief that I was still standing and breathing. But I was shocked as hell as to who rescued me.

"Should I call the police?"

"Naw, let his dumb ass go. He just some young, dumb kid. You all right?"

I took another deep breath and offered a nervous smile. He walked over to me and grabbed my purse off of the ground. He then took the items out of my hands, slipped them in my purse, and handed it to me.

I sat there like I was mute and deaf. Truth was, I didn't know what to say. This was the same man who I had looked down on a few hours ago. And he had just saved my life. I was so grateful to him for doing that. Alone, I didn't have a chance against that man.

"Thank you so much!" I gushed out, grabbing both his hands in mine.

He gave me a look like he was thinking, *Bitch, please*.

Awkward . . .

Nervously, I babbled, "I don't know what I was thinking, leaving work so late and not paying attention to my surroundings . . . And . . ." It continued to be awkward, standing in front of the man I had treated so badly.

To all I said, he replied simply, "It's cool."

"No. It's not. Listen. I should have not treated you so badly. Looked down on you the way I did. But I mean you were really late and—"

"I don't drive around in an *Infiniti* like you do. I got that little busted-ass *Honda* over there. It was giving me a lot of trouble today."

"But the number one excuse people give for being late to an interview or for work is car trouble."

"Has it crossed your mind *why* I'm still here, hours after the punk-ass interview? Think about it, I can't get my car started for shit. That's why I'm still here and was able to save you from getting killed. I called for a ride and they never showed up."

He was making me feel worse by the second.

He chuckled. "You know, I had a nice shirt to wear. When my car stopped on the way here I spilled oil on it. But I figured if I could have gotten at least halfway through the interview, I could have explained that to you. Your dad acted like this was a sure thing because he liked me so much. He said things would be cool with you, not so much a formal interview. But that you liked to screen all future employees first. Still, I wanted to represent myself in a good manner. I really needed the job."

I was such a coldhearted bitch to him, turning my nose up at him for simply trying to get a job. "I'm going to fix this. Look. My dad owns a tow truck company. It's open twenty-four hours. I'll call Sal, the manager, and have them tow your car to your home. You can ride with them, and tomorrow, I will take you to lunch for an impromptu interview." I added with a chuckle, "You can wear whatever you like."

He laughed at that comment. Ten minutes later, Mickey, one of my dad's employees, came and loaded his truck up with Santana's car. Santana gave me his address and number and I went home. I called Dannon to tell him what happened but he didn't answer.

Wow, I thought the whole way to my house, *that man saved my life.*

Chapter 3

Santana lived in a seedy part of Inglewood, a part I would not go to under any circumstances, unless I wanted to get robbed. He stayed in a run-down apartment building that had people hanging out. When I pulled up, I could hear someone blasting loud music inside the building. This new knowledge about his living circumstances now made me feel worse. He was simply a man trying to better himself; thus, he came to us for a job.

I dialed his number and, when he picked up, told him, "Hi. I am outside."

"Cool."

A few minutes later, he stepped out in a crisp white button-down top and a pair of black slacks, and had a pair of dress shoes on as well. *I approve.*

He stood beside the passenger's side of my car. I quickly unlocked the door and he hopped in. As soon as he buckled up, I pulled off and drove toward the freeway.

"What are you playing?" he demanded of me with his lips twisted to the side.

I chuckled. "It's Eric Roberson. Have you ever heard of him? My fiancé got me listening to him. After being on his feet for hours and hours because of his residency, he says his music relaxes him."

When we came to a red light, he took my left hand and examined my ring. He whistled. "You seem worth that, too."

He locked eyes with me when he said that.

I blushed like a schoolgirl and looked down at my lap. I didn't know why, but, coming from him, I took that as a compliment seeing as though I was a straight-up bitch to him. It was cool to see that his perception of me was shifting. All of a sudden, I felt I needed his approval.

When the light changed, I turned and hopped on the 405 South. Our destination was Ruth's Chris Steak House.

Twenty minutes after being seated, Santana had me cracking up as he mimicked how I had acted the day he came in for his interview.

"I was an ultra bitch," I said regretfully.

"It's cool." He cut into his T-bone steak. I was surprised that he didn't seem out of his element in such an expensive place. He ordered his food with ease. His confidence and security were attractive qualities.

I ate a slice of my filet mignon and dipped into my buttery mashed potatoes. "You have a very different name. Where are you from?"

"My mom is black. I'm assuming my dad was Belizean or mixed with Hispanic and black but I don't really know. I grew up Inglewood. I never knew my mother or father. I was given up for adoption at an early age. I was raised by foster parent after foster parent. It was like by the time I made myself at home, I was sent to another home. I been on my own since I was eighteen and have been struggling to make it ever since."

How sad. I couldn't imagine growing up that way. No one should. I was truly lucky to have the type of nurturing and loving parents I had. I always felt like I had a place in my parents' heart and that I mattered beyond compare. I never had to struggle or see them struggle. I never knew what struggle looked like. My little sister and I had always been well loved. We had the best of everything our whole life. We lived in a big, warm home, always had great meals, the best clothes, rode in nice cars, and went to good schools. I think that is why I ended up so successful. But then I understood how someone couldn't. How he could be nearly thirty years old and not have half of what I had?

"Don't get to looking all sad and feeling sorry for me. Life is life, and that was mine. I'm just happy to have one. I'm happy to still be here."

"That's a positive outlook to have," I said.

"Yep. I mean I had a job I loved. The pay was pretty bad. But I was working as a counselor at a teen center not too far from where I live. But due to funding issues, it got closed down. That crushed me."

"A rec center?" I wasn't expecting him to say that.

"You know, a place where inner-city kids and teens can go after school, and in the summer. We offered art, dance, drama, cooking classes, self-esteem, and workshops to them. Well, we used to . . ."

He seemed like a real good person. To work at such a place meant that he had a caring heart.

"I was thinking that after I got another job and on my feet, I could look into opening up my own rec center. Man, that's all I have been thinking about doing, getting incorporated. My old boss promised me she would help me." He ate some of his baked potato. "But you know how you females are."

I chuckled. "Let me guess. You guys started messing around and she broke your heart?"

"Naw. I never messed with her. I just wasn't ready for all of that." His face got suddenly sad. He cleared his throat and got silent for a moment.

I took another bite of my steak, hoping I didn't hit some sort of soft spot. I certainly didn't want to do that. If anything, I wanted to make it up to him for how I had acted, and for him saving my damn life.

"I lost my fiancée about six months ago to breast cancer. So there was no way I was going to get involved with someone else."

Damn. What else is he going to tell me? This man has been through so much! I wondered if I would be able to cope if I had had his life and endured so much pain and tragedy. If I had lost my sweet Dannon.

"That had to be hard for you to go through. I'm so sorry for your loss."

He nodded and ate another piece of his steak. But as he chewed his eyes got watery. His watery eyes went to a cluster of tears that slid down his face. Then he was full-out sobbing at the table.

It broke my heart to see him crying the way that he was. So I pushed my chair closer to him and attempted to offer him comfort by hugging him. I wrapped my arms around him and he continued to cry. I rubbed his back and whispered to him that it would be okay.

Suddenly he pulled away from me. With his head down he said to me, "I can't do this right now. Do you mind if we get out of here?"

"Okay." I figured he no longer had an appetite to eat. No matter how good the food was.

Without a moment's hesitation, he stood to his feet and walked out of the restaurant. I asked our waiter for the bill, paid it, and then joined Santana outside.

The ride back was the complete opposite from when we came, when we had both chatted with each other. We rode back in silence and tear after tear slid down his face, making me feel so bad for him.

When we arrived at his apartment he turned to me and asked, "Why don't you come in and I can get you that resume."

I nodded. We both got out of the car and I followed him to his apartment.

Once we stepped inside, I looked around. "Under primitive" was the best way to describe his apartment. I mean it was. There was one couch, a crate with a small TV on it, and an old, scratched-up dresser. But one thing I could say was that it was spotlessly clean. It had the smell of bleach as if he had just cleaned up before we had left. There were different sculptures sitting on his dresser. I walked closer to them and inspected them. One was a horse, one a gladiator, and a skull.

"Where did you get these?" I asked him.

He was going through a backpack on the floor. He threw back at me, "I made those."

"You did? Wow."

"The skull is made of sand."

He is really talented. You never really know about a person until you take the time to get to know them.

"You should be sharing this with the world," I told him.

"I was. I was teaching the kids I worked with how to make them."

I walked around his living room and spied another sculpture on top of his TV. It was a curvy-looking woman. I picked it up, examined it, and chuckled.

"That one is made of tape. I can pretty much use any type of material, clay, wood, paper, foam, and even cardboard."

I set the sculpture back down. "I've never been really artistic, but I can definitely respect someone who is." I walked over to his couch and sat down. He joined me while he went through a manila folder.

He handed me a copy of his resume. Without looking at it I folded it and slid it into my purse.

There was no need for me to look at it because I was going to hire him. How could I not? I knew he could bring something special to our company. He was an overall nice guy who needed a break. I liked him and I wanted to help him. He had helped me.

As he restacked his papers, a photo fell out and onto the floor, near my feet. I bent down and picked it up. Being nosy, I scanned it before handing it back to him.

"Is that her?"

"Yeah. It is."

"She is really pretty."

"Was."

"Right."

"So, now, what about you? I see you got a rock on your finger but I don't know about the nigga."

"What does that mean?" I asked him.

"You fine as hell, educated. It seems like you finely bred and he just lets you roll around with other niggas?"

"My man trusts me is all." And, truth be told, I wasn't around many other men but family and Dannon. The only guy I was around was my bestie, Justin. But he and my girl Arianna had been my closest friends since preschool. His mother and my mother were friends and gave birth to us around the same time. We had both been singing in our church for as long I could remember. Sometimes we performed songs together.

Justin really wanted to take this singing thing all the way, whereas I didn't have the same aspirations. He was currently a backup singer for Trey Songz. Great gig. While I was happy for him, I was content with what I was doing and eventually becoming a wife. Nevertheless, I loved to sing.

"Keeping it G. If you were my woman you couldn't go to the corner alone." He pierced me with a gaze.

I looked away.

"That's the difference between your nigga and me. I don't play with mine."

For some reason, a jolt went through me as I thought of what it would be like to be with a man like Santana. I didn't want to be having those types of thoughts since I was in love with Dannon but I was. *Shit, I am.* It was one of those things I couldn't really explain to myself. It just felt like some part of me, by the minute, was attaching myself to this man.

"Man. I don't play." He licked his lips.

He moved closer to me so I could feel his breath on my face.

"If you were mine, I would beat that pussy up nonstop."

Another jolt came through me, down below.

"How long you been with that nigga?"

"Since I was fourteen."

"What? You probably ain't had no other dick but his. How can you tell if you want to marry that nigga and be with just him for the rest of your life if you ain't tried no other dick? You ain't ever had another man eat your pussy and you ain't rode another cock?"

I knew this wasn't what I had come here for, but, truth be told, he was right. A couple times in our relationship, I did wonder what it would be like to be with another man before I married Dannon. I would never admit this so I said, "I'm content with my fiancé." But I had, in my mind, toyed with dabbling in another man. I mean, when Dannon and I made love for the first time, we were both virgins.

At this point, his face was filled with desire and his lips grazed mine, due to him being so close, and I didn't stop him. "I would eat that pussy so good you would squirt."

He brazenly and boldly pulled me closer to him. I didn't accept nor decline the intrusion. My heartbeat did speed up at what I was doing. My mind was racing because I knew what

I should do. I knew better. What I was doing to Dannon was wrong. But I closed my eyes and let the kiss go deeper. I parted my lips and let him explore my mouth with his tongue. With it, he teased me in a tantalizing manner. "You want me to eat your pussy from behind?"

I didn't respond, just kept kissing him.

"Seems like you want to see what it feel like. I know I do. You damn near a virgin. I bet your shit is tight." One of his hands had reached between my thighs and a finger was going up and down my love box.

When he kissed me again, I gave into it fully this time. And as the seconds flew, my guilt was getting less and my desire was growing more. He suddenly gripped my thighs possessively and aggressively shoved me back, pushed up my dress, and he slipped his head between my legs. He placed me in bliss as his tongue flicked over my clit. Although I was in love with Dannon, he had been my only partner since I had discovered sex. And Santana was giving it to me in a way that had me yanking at the curls on his head and screaming at the top of my lungs.

Everything about this man had me in a wild-ass frenzy. See, I don't think it was just because of my curiosity to be with another man, or the fact that Santana was a real man. In the short time I had been around him, he had captivated me. I had allowed myself to see him for what he really was. He was a mystery as much as he was an open book. Something about him was trapping me there in that apartment, when I knew I should have gone . . . I couldn't and I didn't wanna. I wanted him to do all the things to my body that he wanted to. So I willed myself to deal with the consequences later. . . .

I opened my legs as he munched away like an expert. I felt my legs stiffen as he stuck a skilled finger in me and started stroking me.

Then he stuck a finger in my mouth, forcing me to taste myself. And I liked doing that. It was not something Dannon would ever make me do. But I enjoyed it. Then he made a fist and rubbed it up and down my shaft in a frenzy. I screamed at the top of my lungs. My pussy started making a gurgling sound and fluid shot out of me into Santana's face.

He chuckled at me and went back to eating my pussy. The next thing I knew, he had me on all fours and his dick was stabbing my pussy, doing an assault on it like it was on punishment.

I was yelling and could feel myself nutting. Abruptly, he pulled out and got up. Disappointed, as the sensations slowly begin to leave me, I watched him sit on the edge of his couch.

"Get over here," he commanded.

I obeyed. He had me position myself so that my back was to him and my legs were on the outside of his legs.

"Okay. Get the dick."

I slowly eased myself down on him inch by inch. The pleasure was good but it hurt at the same time because he was so damn much bigger than Dannon. I had to get used to the size before I rode him faster. I rode him slowly and moaned deeply at how good it felt. I threw my head back and moaned loudly.

"What you crying for? You wanted this dick so take it!"

His hands gripped my waist and he shoved me down his shaft. My walls widened and I cried out at the pleasure. I rode him at a faster pace. He gripped my breasts in his hands, squeezing my nipples. Then, he slapped me on my bottom, telling me to get off of him. I did. He shoved me until I was on my knees. He got behind me again and was humping me doggie style.

Suddenly, he jumped up, sat on the backs of my legs, and gripped his hands around my neck. He whispered in my ear, "Check this out, bitch, today and every day after today, you mine and this is my pussy. So tell your fiancé he gotta kick rocks. You understand me?" He eased back down and stuck his dick back into my pussy all while still holding my neck.

He plowed deep into me, causing me to bite my bottom lip.

"You understand?" He jabbed me again. "*Huh?*"

"Yes!"

From that point on, my purpose for life was forever changed.

Chapter 4

Two Months Later . . .

Something about him . . . He had turned my
normal world upside down. My daily motivation
was keeping him happy. The affair I was having
with Santana lasted a good month before Dannon
found out about it. Initially, I told myself that my
desire and attraction for him was just about sex.
He was a very attractive man, with a big penis,
and I thought I would get over it. That it was
merely a woman's curiosity because I had only
been with one man and about to marry that man.
Who knows . . . Maybe it started out that way. A
means for me to sex another discreetly. That day
we did what we did, I was already in his house,
so who would find out? But I just couldn't end it
there. Each day, I wanted to be around him more,
like he was my drug. I started getting clumsy with
him, ignoring Dannon's calls, not being available
to him, and missing our dates. This was because

the more I saw Santana the less interest I had in seeing or being around Dannon. That meant sex as well. It became more mundane with Dannon. Boring. With Santana we did wild, freaky, new things I knew Dannon wouldn't be down for. We even filmed ourselves, watched it, and made love again. Maybe some people thought that was dumb of me. But for me I had learned long ago that time didn't make a friend and time certainly didn't make a partner. Even though I had known Santana for a short time frame, my feelings for him were way more intense than the feelings I now felt for Dannon.

I knew people wouldn't understand so I didn't bother going to Dannon's funeral, although it enraged my parents, who both went. Even my sister went. She told me I should be ashamed of myself and asked me what I was on. Seeing as she had come completely undone her first year at Spelman, she was no one to judge. I had seen the pictures on Facebook. As far as Santana . . . I couldn't explain the feelings; they just were there the way they were there. To sum it up in a sentence, I had a loss of feeling for Dannon and the instant outpour of emotions for Santana.

I felt bad that Dannon had taken his life and I wished I had done things differently. But I didn't want to be around people pointing the finger at me like I had killed him. Dannon killing himself was completely unexpected, let me tell you. I knew I couldn't blame myself, only a fool would. He didn't have to take his life. True enough, we had been together for ten years, but he could have just moved on. I wasn't going to make myself miserable feeling bad because he killed himself. How was I to know he would go there? Dannon never appeared to be the type of man to have suicidal tendencies. He always seemed happy and never seemed to be down. It couldn't have just been about me. But everyone seemed to blame me for it. Who really knew what was going on in his head? It was easier to blame someone, I suppose, but I wasn't going to blame myself. That's one of the main reasons I didn't go to the funeral. I refused to be persecuted.

Santana told me from jump that to be his woman there were certain rules I had to follow. He was a man who needed to be cared for properly or I would lose him to the next bitch. My man had goals and I needed to make sure he accomplished them. He said I needed to hold him down. So I bought him a new wardrobe, with top-of-the-line tags. He stopped working for my daddy and enrolled in school. I agreed to pay his bills so all he had to do was focus on going to class and studying. He was studying to be an auto mechanic. He was happy to have a woman to hold him down. He said I needed to make sure he was always well fed. He said good food would always keep him potent and make the sex good. His meals typically consisted of steak or seafood that I either prepared or went out and got. I never bought cheap food or fast food. He liked gourmet. And I had no problem delivering. He also expected me to give him the best head at the drop of a hat. He said that's where dumb women fucked up and lost their man, because they didn't want to go down. "Remember," he told me, "What you won't do another woman will. And I ain't got no problem letting her, if you ain't trying to take care of home." Well, he didn't have to worry about that! I put it down with my head game. I learned from him how to do it just right. I also had to be ready at all times to ride his cock and take it however he wanted me to. In fact, I had to put him first in everything. If I was at work and he called me saying he needed some loving, I had no problem leaving my job, going to him, and then going back to work with a smile on my face. The only thing I didn't do was let him move in. I told him it would have to be marriage first. I didn't even live with Dannon. He never responded to that. I was glad he didn't because, truthfully, I didn't want to shack and we needed a little more time before we thought about marriage.

I walked into Santana's apartment and sat down. When I called him and told him I was on the way, he said he was just getting in the shower. I moved his wallet and cell phone over, sat down on the couch, and put my purse down next to me. His cell phone started ringing. I snatched it up to give it to him when I saw it said that Reina was calling. I wondered who that was. But since our relationship was still fresh, I didn't see him cheating on me. Look what he had and what I was offering him: all my love and faithfulness. I had got him hired with my father, cosigned for him to get a new car: a Chrysler 300. He had no reason to do me wrong. I ignored it and set the phone back down. He was in the shower getting ready for church. I was taking him there for the first time to meet my family.

Our church was called The Rock and was located in Long Beach, in the Traffic Circle. I had been going there for as long as I could remember. My mother was the choir director and my father was one of the deacons. After service, my mother always made a huge dinner, and that would be the opportunity for them to get acquainted with Santana.

We arrived to the church a little late. After Santana was seated, I rushed up to the stage and stood next to my best friend and roommate, Arianna. My mother was in front of the choir and gave me a weird look for my lateness. I ignored it and joined them in singing "Going Down to Yonder." The song was almost finished. Once everyone clapped, the entire choir sat down and I was left standing because I was supposed to sing a solo this week. Truth was, I hadn't really practiced. But I was pretty much a natural at singing so I knew I would be able to pull it off.

I closed my eyes as the band played the tune and I let my voice take off:

> "*I had enough heartache and enough headaches.*
>   *I've had so many ups and downs.*
>   *Don't know how much more I can take.*
>   *See, I decided that I cried my last tears yesterday.*"

People were shouting, "Thank you, Jesus!"
My dad yelled, "Sing that song, baby!"
By the time I got to the second chorus, my mother was crying. It was always like that.

People in my church always got emotional when I sang.

I was so into the song too that I started tearing up as well. My mother always said that when I opened my mouth to sing, it was one of the greatest gifts the world could be blessed with. I was three years old when my church discovered that I could sing. I had been on that stage ever since.

I sang the chorus and some people started standing and waving their arms. But the person I wanted approval from was missing from his seat: Santana. However, I knew I could be heard even if he was in the restroom. I closed out the song with the last lines:

> *"Here ain't nothing too hard for my God, no.*
> *Any problems that I have.*
> *He's greater than them all."*

Tears slid down my face at the last line. I made my voice rip into the last line. "So I decided that I cried my last tears yesterday."

I got a standing ovation like I normally did. Santana came out of the restroom and sat down.

The pastor started his sermon and my friend whispered in my ear. "So finally I get to meet this Santana, huh? The one who you are so into you wouldn't even bother coming to your fiancé's funeral?"

I pierced her with a glare. "Arianna, not now. I've had enough backlash from my family. I *don't* need it from you."

"Really, Alexis, what are you thinking? You know that Dannon's parents are members of this church. How could you?"

"You act like I pulled the trigger!" I whispered furiously. "I am sorry that Dannon ended his life but I won't be held responsible for it by you or his parents. I like Santana and he is here to stay no matter what you or anyone else says. And, besides, they haven't been back to this church in weeks."

"Would you? They probably want to avoid you at all costs! You were, after all, the apple of their son's eye and you didn't even go show your respects to his family. I can't see them ever showing their face here again or anywhere near you."

I hoped they didn't come back. I could do without that awkward moment when we came face to face. I was glad they stopped coming to this church. When they were contacted by one of the ushers they said they no longer wished to be members.

Aside from how I felt about the backlash, the day of Dannon's funeral, I was also too engulfed in Santana's dick. We had tried anal sex that day. And it felt so good I wanted more and more. I was too bent out of shape to show my face at anyone's funeral. I snapped at Arianna, "Did I plan to go? Yes! But I got wrapped up into something. I couldn't!"

My mother looked our way. I tried to smile. "Drop it, Arianna. Be a friend and don't judge." I quickly put my head into my HTC phone to follow along and read the scripture.

The whole time my best friend mumbled, "Umph." She continued to stare and shake her head at me. I tuned her out.

When church services were over, I went over to where Santana was sitting and kissed him on the lips. "How was it?" I asked him.

"Too fucking long."

I put a finger to my lips and studied him. He looked disinterested. But, then, I learned that not everyone was into church. Maybe it was something that I could introduce him to and he would soon have a passion for learning the Word as well. Dannon had always had a love for Christ. It was good for your mate to be spiritual and since I wanted Santana to be my man, I had to help him get there. I knew that I could.

As people exited the church, I slipped my hand in Santana's and told him, "Come on. You can meet my mother, sister, and the pastor."

"We going to eat over there ain't we? I can meet them there. Forget your pastor. He's boring as fuck."

"Okay. And shh about my pastor." I giggled and tapped him on the shoulder as he guided me out of the church. I loved my pastor and I knew eventually Santana would as well. And yes, church did take eons and eons to be done. But I was used to it.

We made our way over to my car; I went toward the passenger side. As I waited for Santana to unlock the car, someone tapped me on the back. I smiled and turned around. I was shocked when I came face to face with Dannon's mother. I gasped and nervously stuttered over my words.

"I just came here to see if it was true. You had the audacity to bring him to this church where my son used to worship. He is part of the reason my son is no longer here."

I snapped my head back. "You don't even know him."

An audience slowly formed around us in the parking lot and I could hear whispers. Church people liked gossip just like anyone else.

"Don't insult my intelligence, you little bitch! I know he is Santana, the same man who was there screwing you the day my son came in! What happened to you, Alexis? You were the light of my son's life! He was so in love with you. How could you do this to him? You didn't even have enough respect to come to his funeral!" Her hand flew back and she slapped the shit out of me.

My eyes teared up and one of my hands went to my face.

"Old lady, get the fuck out of here!" Santana shouted.

"You bastard!" She held her hand up to strike him but he grabbed it and shoved her roughly to the ground. She fell hard and she skinned one of her knees.

"How can you do that to a woman?" Mr. Waters from the congregation demanded. He bent over to help her up.

"You old dumb-ass bitch."

"Hey!" Mrs. McGee shouted as she rushed toward us. "Watch your mouth. I'm going to get your mother. I can't believe you are keeping company like him and are letting him disrespect Mrs. Reed that way!" She was outraged and stormed off, shaking her head.

I put my head down. But I agreed with Santana. Dannon's mother was out of line. It was not my nor Santana's fault her son had killed himself.

He tossed a hand at her and said, "Get in the car, baby."

I did as he said. I didn't like all the foul language Santana had used but I appreciated him defending my honor. Especially since everyone else was making me out to be the bad guy. People would just have to accept the fact that I was down with Santana. To love me was to love him.

Chapter 5

My parents live in a huge six-bedroom upstairs and downstairs home in Bixby Knolls. When Santana and I arrived, the whole house smelled like collard greens and sweet potato pie.

My parents' house was huge. Over the years we had added on. As much as I had always loved my parents' home, I had moved out and into one of my father's properties with my bestie Arianna a couple years ago. My parents didn't want me to leave but I felt it was time for me to branch out on my own. And even though I didn't pay rent there, I felt living on my own gave me some independence and made me more responsible. I wondered *if* my sister graduated college would she leave the nest or stay with my parents. She would probably stay.

"This is a bad-ass house," Santana said.

"There is where I grew up. Maybe one day we will have a house just as big."

"Yeah, maybe." His tone was doubtful.

He sat down on the huge brown suede sectional and I went into the kitchen to see where my mother was. She was there with my nana. Both were cooking.

"Hey, ladies."

My grandmother stopped what she was doing and kissed me on my cheek. My mother ignored me.

"Mommy. You need any help?"

"No. But it seems like you do."

I narrowed my eyes at her, confused. My mother was very pretty and looked youthful to be in her fifties. She was light brown with deep brown eyes, high cheekbones, and straight white teeth. We were the same height, had the same frames: big breasts, small waists, and we were hippy. While my mother had her hair cut short, my sister and I kept our real shoulder-length hair flat ironed and silky, always parted down the middle. My sister and I were often told that we both looked a lot like Laura London. I was fine with the comparison. She was a movie star, after all.

"Alexis!"

"Yes, Mom?"

"Pay close attention when I am talking to you. Your father and I worked very hard to give you and your sister the life that we have. And what the hell are you doing with this man? You had a great guy and you seem to have forgotten that just thirty days ago, he killed himself. And you are parading this guy in front of the church? He should be in jail after the way he treated Clare."

"He was protecting me. Clare slapped me."

"If I were Dannon's mother I would have done a whole lot more. I would have whipped your ass!"

"Mom!" My mother never spoke to me in that way. It was offensive.

"I'm not going to handle you with kid gloves when I feel like you are making bad choices. You should have shown them more respect than to do what you did."

"Oh, Mother, please. Why go to the funeral when it was clear that everyone, including you, blames Santana and me for his death?"

My grandmother was mixing something in a bowl. "Sandy. Let the girl make her own mistakes. She will learn soon enough on her own."

My mother ignored her and started chopping an onion. "I know you didn't pull the trigger, but Dannon was obviously very hurt that he caught you with another man when you two were supposed to marry. That man loved you. And he was a good man. You should have done better by him than you did. You should have broken it off or stopped seeing that man you call yourself crazy about. But to carry on for a month with that man behind Dannon's back, knowing the pressure he was under, was just wrong. And to have the man in your house!"

"Well, I can't change the past. And I really need you to give Santana a chance. You keep comparing him to Dannon. He is an underdog. He wasn't raised with a silver spoon in his mouth. And, Mother, you know what they say about underdogs. They come out on top. He is in school right now, studying to be an auto mechanic. And you always loved a man good with his hands, like Daddy. So, Mommy, I'm merely following in your footsteps. I think he's going to be something great. You will see, Mommy. And if you just give him a chance you will love him like I already feel that I do."

At this point it seemed that my mother had tuned me out. She offered no response and was now checking on a pot on the stove. It was fine by me, because at the end of the day, I was going to make my own decisions whether she supported them or not. And her focus on the food cooking gave me the opportunity to go back out to the living room and hang out with Santana until Sunday dinner was done.

***

Just as we sat down to eat, I tried to introduce my mother to Santana and everyone else. My mother was so cold to him, stiffly shaking his hand before taking her seat at the dinner table. My father had already met Santana and even though he was no longer working for him, he was pleasant to him, and so were my grandmother and grandfather. My sister didn't even acknowledge him. But that didn't last for long.

We all sat across from each other at our huge dinner table in the dining room. I squeezed Santana's hand under the table. We feasted on baked salmon, roasted Cornish hens, a super tender and well-flavored roast beef, asparagus tips that Santana almost gagged on, garlic new potatoes, collard greens, and vegetable medley. For dessert my nana had made sweet potato pie, pound cake, and a five-layer chocolate cake. As good as the food was, there was so much tension at the table. My sister sat there chewing on her food and shaking her head at me. My dad was neutral but my mother continued to stare at Santana with a piercing gaze, all while my grandmother took the opportunity to stuff herself with food she didn't need due to her diabetes. But ever since my grandfather had been diagnosed with Alzheimer's, she had been using food for comfort. Normally, my mother would monitor her but her attention was on my new man. My grandfather acted like he didn't even know who my sister and I were. I just hoped the attack I received at church, when Dannon's mother had gone off on me, would be the last one. But my bitchy sister continued to sit at the table with a foul expression on her face like she had just drank some buttermilk. So I didn't think the war was over. I knew someone was going to go in on me during dinner. I gave her a look that said, "Don't start," but it didn't stop her from drilling me. She was such a spoiled, snobby bitch. Ugh! Just because we were pretty and wealthy didn't give any of us the right to act like we were the shit.

"Alexis! I'm scratching my head trying to figure out how you can have the nerve to bring this man in our house, to our dinner table, after you lost your fiancé. What the hell is wrong with you?"

My mother's fork dropped. "Bria," she hissed. "Watch your mouth. You have adults at the table."

"I'm grown too."

I narrowed my eyes to slits at her. I had never disrespected my mother like she just had. And, secondly, where the hell did she get off questioning me? There were videos of her all over

WorldStarHiphop.com, busting it open and kissing girls! Not to mention her horrific Facebook page.

"It's none of your—"

"It is! Dannon was like a big brother to me. And you've got this thug at our table."

"Bria, stop it!" I fired.

She frowned and crossed her arms under her chest, giving me the stink eye.

Santana threw his head back and laughed at her. She then turned her stink eye on him.

"You lucky you a cutie, else I'd make you cry, little girl."

She gave him a weird look at him calling her "cute." I knew he wasn't flirting with her. He was just saying she was cute because she was my little sister.

"Which projects did you crawl out of?"

"Don't be a little bitch!" I yelled.

"Alexis! Bria!" my mother shouted.

She flung her shoulder-length hair to the side. "Well, someone has to take that stick out of her ass, or something else that is obviously stuck up Miss Prissy, with the dumb moves you're making."

My mother and I gasped.

Santana chuckled.

The sound of a fist hitting the table made everyone except for Santana and my grandfather jump.

We all looked at my daddy, who had fire in his eyes. And he was normally a calm man.

"Listen. That's enough. You two girls need to watch your mouth and how you speak to each other. I didn't raise you two that way. Yes. It is sad that Dannon died." My father pulled off his glasses and continued. "I loved Dannon like a son. And I'm sure Alexis didn't plan on things going the way they did. But we as her family need to respect her wishes."

I exhaled. "Thank you, Daddy."

My sister continued to stare at me and shake her head.

Santana pushed his chair back and stood. "Where is the head?" Everyone looked confused, so he said, "Bathroom."

"Down the hall to the right," I told him. He walked out of the room.

"But, Daddy, she is dumb. You wasted all that money educating her and look at the dumb decisions she is making with this—"

"That's it! I can't take her anymore."

I pulled my napkin off my lap and tossed it on the table before pushing my chair back and standing to my feet. I walked out of the dining room toward the bathroom Santana was in and knocked on the door.

"Damn. What?"

"Baby. Meet me at the car outside." I turned to walk to the living room and the hell out of my parents' house before I killed my little sister. We were always so close but she was being such a judgmental bitch. I didn't judge her with all her mishaps she was doing in college. When I got to the door and reached for the knob I heard someone call my name.

I turned around and saw my mother walking toward me with a Bible in her hand.

Oh, Lord.

She placed it in the air as if in surrender. "I didn't come to berate you at all. Just listen to me. I want to show you something." She turned the Bible to Proverbs 4:23. She put her manicured index finger on a line and said calmly, "Read that, baby. That all I need you to do and then you can go."

"Mom."

"What does it say?" she insisted in a stern voice.

I took a deep breath and read it. "It says . . . 'Guard your heart above all else, for it determines the course of your life.'"

"What do you think that means, baby?"

"Mom! Are we going to have Bible Study right now, like really?"

She closed her eyes and nodded. "Okay. But just think about what it says, Alexis. And if you have a question about it, call me."

"I will, Mom." I gave her a hug and opened the door. Before stepping out, I paused and gave her one final look. She stood there wringing her hands as if she was filled with so much dread. She really didn't need to be. I knew how to take care of myself. I was perfectly fine. I knew Santana was rough around the edges but other than that, he was just fine for me. Gosh. I had always been taught that it didn't matter where you start but where you ended up. Santana would be just fine. He had me to shape and mold him into the best man he could be.

I walked to my car, opened the driver's door, and sat down. A few minutes later, Santana came walking toward the car and was talking on his cell phone. He had the HTC. I got it for him; before that he had a Metro PCS phone. I told him he needed an upgrade. When he saw me in the car he cut the convo short and placed his phone in his pocket. I wondered who he was talking to and why he couldn't have the conversation in front of me.

Before I could ask him who he was talking to he slipped in the passenger seat and said, "Your family is a fucking trip! Y'all may have money, but all y'all got issues."

"No family is perfect," I said defensively, making a mental note to ask him later who he was talking to.

"But, shit, your granddaddy didn't say a single word. He acted like he didn't know how to fucking talk. And your grandmamma acted like she was going to eat herself into a grave."

"Well, since my grandfather was diagnosed with Alzheimer's, she has been very depressed and eating more. She used to be small like my mother."

"Whose parents are they?"

"My mother's. My father's parents live in West Virginia."

It was like he stopped listening as I talked. Like he went into a daze.

"Santana?"

He refocused his eyes on me. "And your sister." He shook his head.

She had pissed me off so bad today. I probably wouldn't have defended her to anyone. I loved her to death but she was changing. She always had been wild and a little loose. But she always had respect for me as her big sister.

"Your mom cracked me up, though. She seems bougie as hell. She reminds me of you. But I'm going to break you up out of that shit. The only one that seems halfway decent is your father."

My mind went back to the phone call. "So who was that you were talking to when you were walking to the car?"

"No one," was the quick reply.

I was silent, not buying it because he was speaking to someone. His quick reply and refusal to tell me who it was caused a little alarm. I made a mental note to look in his phone and see if it was the same girl whose number I saw in his phone earlier. I wanted to question him further but I didn't want to argue because I wanted to make love.

"Aye, baby. Come here."

"What?"

"Go down and suck on Lethal." That was the nickname for his penis.

"Baby. Can't we wait until we get home?"

He pulled it out of his pants. It was so big it slapped against his stomach. "I want it now."

I sighed and knew if I didn't do what he wanted he wouldn't let me come over, and I always feared that if I left him wanting he would go to another. Other women should have thought that way too. That was why their men were cheating on them. That's probably why Arianna's man had cheated on her.

I looked around the long driveway. No one was outside and they were probably enjoying dessert now. My sister's Charger was parked next to my Infiniti. Then there was my mother's Benz and my dad's Beemer. I figured no one would be outside anyhow.

So I bent my head down and started sucking on my baby.

"Damn. Shit, baby."

I bobbed my head up and down on his dick. I made sure I kept my mouth wet. I used my hand to rub up and down his shaft like he had taught me to. He was pushing his body up from the seat, like he was entering me. I held on tight and continued to use my jaws to suck him. When he came, I swallowed all of it.

Suddenly out of nowhere, Santana started laughing.

Confused, I peered up at his face and asked before I even got a chance to wipe my face, "What?" Cum leaked from my chin.

He pointed out the window.

I sat up, looked out the window, and saw my sister staring back at me, near her car. She started shaking her head.

Embarrassed, I put my head down.

Chapter 6

After Santana dozed off to sleep, I went through his phone to see who the last call was from. And, sure enough, the caller's name was Reina. Instantly, I wondered who she was. The fact that she was a female and he was so dismissive when I asked who he was talking to made me furious. Logically speaking, I knew he had no family out here so she being blood related was not a possibility. I told myself that it could possibly be someone from his school or old job. But I was unable to convince myself that that was where he knew her from. I needed to know just who the woman was. I needed 100 percent confirmation and nothing less. . . .

When I went to work the next day, I could not for any reason focus. I ignored my office phone as well as my email. Same applied for doing paperwork. I dialed Reina's number. Santana was my man and I had a right to know who she was. I didn't want to ask him because then I would be telling that I went through his phone. I didn't want him to feel that I didn't trust him.

He had always told me that that was an open door for him to cheat. "If you think I'm doing the shit why the fuck not do it?" he always said.

So without any more hesitation, I dialed the number and took a deep breath. I felt super nervous as the phone rang. Part of me hoped that she wouldn't pick up. And if she did . . . What was she going to tell me? That she was sleeping with Santana? That he was in love with her and she as well? It would positively crush me. An image of Santana panting over another naked woman filled my eyes. I shook my head to block the image out.

A female answered, "Hello?"

My heart sped up. Thinking of a lie, quickly, I said, "Hi. I found this number in my boyfriend's pants pocket."

"Then, bitch, put it back!"

I gasped.

Then the call ended.

Now I was more curious as to who the bitch was. The nerve of her to hang up in my face! I started surfing the Web to see if I could find out a way to get a person's address with merely their phone number. Granted, it was never something I ever had to do with Dannon, but Santana was a different man. I never had any doubt in my mind as to what Dannon was doing when I wasn't around. Don't get me wrong, I felt Santana was just as good of a man as Dannon was, minus the silver spoon in his mouth, but the thing was, our relationship was so fresh, so new. Maybe he had some loose ends he hadn't quite yet tied. My loose end was Dannon, and that loose end was now tied because he had died. But had he still been alive, who was to say he wouldn't have been calling or popping up to beg me to go back to him? Had Dannon still been alive, I would have broken things off with him for Santana. It could be the same scenario for Santana. Maybe he had broken things off with her and she was still begging him back. Or he had one foot out and one foot in because he didn't know how to end it with her. But to be sure, I needed to find out on my own.

I dialed Arianna's number.

"Hello?"

I ignored the irritation in her voice. "Arianna. What was the name of that site you used to track down the chick Will was cheating on you with?"

I frown as I was greeted with silence. She was my bestie and if anyone should be upset it should have been me, not her, after how she brutally judged me at church.

"Well?" I snapped.

She sighed into the phone. That was it! She had tried my patience.

"Never mind!" I hung up in her goddamned face. "Self-centered bitch!" Madly, I typed away on the computer for a good twenty minutes, until I discovered what site it was. It was called Spokeo. I paid twenty-five dollars for the service and put the number in. The shit was amazing. Reina and Trisha Brown popped up. It had all their info: where they lived, how much money they made. It was insane! The one I was concerned with was Reina because she was, after all, the bitch calling my man.

I jotted down all the information I needed. She lived in Compton, on Bullis Road. I called my dad and left a message, telling him I would be out of the office for the rest of the day.

I put the paper in my purse, grabbed my cell and keys, and locked up my office. Since my office was located in Lakewood—across from a shopping center that had various restaurants like Pick Up Stix, Cornerstone Bakery, and Cold Stone, and a cleaners—I was not far at all from Compton. I could take either the freeway or the streets. To avoid traffic, I decided to get to Atlantic Avenue and take that all the way to Compton. Once I made it to her street, I drove slowly, scanning for her address. I found it and parked across the street from her yellow house that had a huge picture window. I looked around disdainfully at all the raggedy apartments and run-down houses on her street. Yes, she had a house, but look where it was. After inspecting her home further, I saw that it looked pretty shabby as well.

I turned on my satellite radio and waited for any type of movement, someone coming to or leaving the house.

It was well over an hour that I still found myself parked out there. I needed to use the bathroom and my throat was dry from thirst. But still I waited. I wondered who she was and what she would look like. Was she competition for me? Again, I asked myself, what was the extent of their relationship? If there really was one. The thing about Santana was that he was far more manly and sophisticated than Dannon. There was still a mystery that surrounded Santana. At times I liked it and at times, like this, I didn't.

After twenty more minutes of waiting, I could no longer hold my bladder. I silently asked myself why I was going through with this nonsense. I didn't know if I was taking that stance now because it was how I sincerely felt or because I had to pee.

I started my ignition, put my car in drive, and pulled off while simultaneously snapping my seat belt. I drove up the street pretty fast, preparing to make a left turn, but a red Impala turned down the street quickly, blasting Nicki Minaj's "Stupid Hoe." She made her turn so fast and wide she nearly collided with my car.

I hit my brakes quickly and placed a hand over my heart, which started beating rapidly.

She put her head out the window and yelled in a ghetto voice, "Bitch. Watch where the fuck you going!"

I fearfully looked away and waited for her to drive past me so I could turn and get off that street before her ghetto ass hurled more insults my way. "And they wonder why white people look down on us," I mumbled to myself. I eyed her in my rearview mirror. I gasped when she pulled into the driveway of the house I had been watching. I wondered if it was her or Trisha. Spokeo also said that Reina Brown had two kids who lived with her. It didn't mention anything about Trisha having kids. I backed up slightly and watched her get out of the car, as two kids got out of the back seat. Before she got a chance to look my way again I skidded down the street. I was definitely going to confront Santana about this.

As I drove, tears were in my eyes and I believed the worst about her and my man: that she was having an affair with him. "It wasn't supposed to go this way," I told myself miserably, as all sorts of scenarios played out in my head of him and her. I drove to the 710 freeway and jumped on it in a frenzy. I fought my way through traffic, switching to the 91, then the 110, and went over to Santana's pad.

Chapter 7

One thing is for sure, I thought. *He doesn't have that woman's number for nothing.* Once I got to his apartment, I parked my car on the street and marched up to his door. I didn't bother knocking. I simply opened the door and stormed inside, yelling, "Santana! I need to talk to . . ."

My voice trailed off when I saw him look at me, surprised, and two more visitors sitting on the couch. I studied them quickly. They were two dudes, both with long dreads in their hair. The older one was light brown with dreads so long they were pulled back in a ponytail, while the younger brown-skinned guy's dreads went to his shoulders.

I stuttered, "Ahhh."

Santana looked at me with an annoyed look on his face.

"I'm sorry. I didn't know you were having company."

Neither of the dreaded men even acknowledged me. So I didn't bother to acknowledge them.

"Me out. Chu know where me be posted," the older one said. They both stood to their feet and exited Santana's apartment.

"All right," Santana said. "I'll hit you up."

Once the door closed, I turned to Santana, not having a good feeling about the two men. "Who are they?"

"Man." He gave me an agitated look. "Fuck out of mine."

"What?" I asked, even though I had heard him pretty much say to stay out of his business.

"You heard what I said. You ain't all in mine and you ain't never going to be."

I sat down on the couch, put my face in my hands, and started crying. It had no effect on him. He just stared at me blankly; in comparison, Dannon would have comforted me. But that was just making me a baby. Santana was turning me into a real woman. A stronger woman.

"Are you seeing someone else?" I demanded. When he didn't respond I continued to blabber, "Because I looked in your phone and saw a number and I called it and she said . . ." Blah, blah, blah. I told him all that I had done, except for looking her up and going to the girl's house, despite the fact that I told myself I wasn't going to even mention anything to him. But I needed to know. Plain and simple.

His head fell back and he laughed. "So you see a number in my phone and you do some PI type of shit. Man. Your family should have put you in therapy, girl. You worried about a bitch who is all in your head who you ain't never seen me with. Your nigga right here though." He grabbed his dick. "And he hard, and he hungry."

I got defensive. "I didn't make it up. The number is in your phone."

"That bitch is about business. Plain and simple. She goes to my school. She wanted me to talk to her little brother about going to school and staying out of trouble. I ain't never been to her house or nothing like that shit you talking about."

I immediately felt bad for the spying. Here he was doing something nice and I was thinking he was screwing her. How stupid I was!

"It's other things in the world to worry about besides bitches. Your ass needs to be worrying about yo' nigga and what my needs are."

He was right and all I could do was nod, feeling instant relief that it wasn't what I thought it was.

"Come here."

I walked over to him and stood in front of him. He sat on the edge of the couch and rubbed his hands up and down my butt, turning me on in an instant.

"And suppose I'm fucking somebody else. What were you going to do about it?" He rubbed a finger between my legs, looking at me with a cocky expression. I was getting wet because of what he was doing and the way he was looking at me.

I responded by moaning.

"Let me answer that for you. Nothing. Girl, you addicted to this dick. You ain't going nowhere."

He was right. I was addicted to him and sometimes I felt as though I couldn't handle this shit, that it was just too much, because day by day, I felt myself sinking deeper and deeper into him. Just earlier, I had fear and dread that he was seeing someone else and now I was convinced that he wasn't. But still, I wondered, if he really was seeing another woman, would I be able to let him go? Probably not. That was what scared me: the fact that I felt I would have an inability to leave him. I pushed those thoughts out of my head and went into the kitchen.

I made him chicken breasts stuffed with bacon, bell peppers, scallions, and cheese. I peeled and boiled some potatoes, mashed them, and mixed them with some cream cheese, real butter, salt and pepper. I also made some string beans mixed with onion and sausage. I had put a bottle of Moët in the freezer so it was perfectly chilled when I brought his food to him.

He ate with relish and it made me feel good to see I had pleased him after I had questioned him about the girl. I was so glad my mother had taught my sister and me how to cook and bake. She always told me that just because we had some money didn't mean that we should neglect those two things. They were attributes that all women should have. All men wanted their women to know how to make a home-cooked meal.

I rubbed his shoulders while he ate and when he was done, I put his plate in the kitchen, washed the dishes, and put the leftover food away.

I stripped down and sat on the couch, anticipating what was to come next.

He came and stood in front of me, asking, "You know you got work to do right?"

I nodded. Thing was, I loved pleasing him. He dropped his pants and I quickly kneeled in front of him and proceeded to suck and lick on his dick until I felt his body tense up. When he had enough, he pulled his dick out of my mouth.

He told me get on all fours. Once I did, he wiped saliva onto my anal hole. I knew we were about to have anal sex. Dannon had never had anal sex with me. He said it was very unsafe and that it tore skin. I chalked that up to Dannon being paranoid because now, I saw no harm in it with Santana. I bore down at the initial pain of my tight skin loosening up. I gritted my teeth as the full ten inches of him slid into me. And I took all of it, counting down in my head as the pain subsided and he was putting it on me in a way that was driving me insane and felt so damn good. I screamed at the top of my lungs and gripped the carpet with my fingernails.

He pumped me roughly. "You like this shit, huh?"

"Yes," I moaned.

"You ain't had anyone give it to you like me, huh?"

"No. No one."

He jabbed me with his dick. "You ain't going to leave me, huh?"

He sped up the tempo, making me drown out his words with my screams of passion. He grabbed my ponytail and yanked it as he rode me.

"You hear me fucking talking to you?"

"No! No!" And I meant that shit. Every syllable of it.

He laughed. "You done met your match with me."

I knew I had slipped deeper just in that moment.

Chapter 8

I was on cloud nine the next day at work. I was thinking about how good I enjoyed myself at Santana's house. Try as I might, I couldn't stop thinking about that man. That's how my days had been the past couple months. Jesus Christ, that man! I was on pins and needles for my day to end so I could rush over to see him.

After doing a little paperwork, I dialed Santana's cell phone. After the third ring, a female picked it up and said, "Hello?"

Instantly, my heart started beating fast and my hands started shaking. I dropped the phone, bent over to retrieve it, and bumped my head on my desk.

"Shit!"

I couldn't stop my fingers from shaking as I dialed his number again. This time someone picked up but I was greeted with silence.

I assumed it was him. "Santana! Say something!" I shouted into the phone. When I was greeted with silence, I said, "I'm coming over there!"

I grabbed my purse keys and cell phone. I locked up quickly and ran to my car.

Once I closed the space between myself and my car, I heard my name called. I turned around and spotted Marisol, the manager for our complex in Cerritos.

She rushed up to me breathlessly. "I'm glad I caught you. I—"

I cut her off. "Now is not a good time."

"I just wanted to drop off the rent deposits—"

"Now is not a good fucking time!" I unlocked my door and hopped in my car. When she stared at me in shock I said, "Get the fuck out of my way," and pulled off.

When I made it to Santana's house, I discovered he wasn't there. I was going to call his phone but thought smarter and went over to the house in Compton. And sure enough when I got there I saw his Chrysler 300 parked next her Impala. If he had never been to her house before what was he doing there now? I was so disappointed in him being dishonest with me.

I parked on the street and got out of my car with fury. My feelings were so hurt from his deception. I stood by my car and stared into the picture window. Santana was sitting on her couch and the same girl who had cursed me out the other day was on his lap, kissing him. I crossed the street and the closer I got to her house, I could see broken pieces of bricks near her driveway. I walked back over to the bricks and picked a half cracked brick and hurled it with all my might at the picture window. I watched the girl jump off his lap and run away. Santana stood and looked out the broken window at me. His eyes widened in surprise.

"You lying bastard!" I yelled.

I turned and walked toward my car, crying loudly. I opened the driver's door. Before I could get completely in my car the girl ran outside. My eyes widened as she raised a gun and started firing shots in my direction. I screamed and jumped into my car and closed the door. I didn't even buckle my seat belt. I started the car and drove off before she had a chance to kill me. My heart was pounding wildly as I sped away, fearing one of the bullets would claim me.

I bawled and sped over to my mother's house. I was so hurt by Santana. How could he get himself out of this one? He was in her home and they were kissing. What excuse could he give me? It was what it was. He was cheating with her.

"Such a liar!" I yelled as I continued to drive. I couldn't stop crying. I wanted to be with Santana.

But he had turned my emotions upside down with his hurt.

I pulled in my parents' driveway, thankful that my mother's Benz was parked, meaning she was home. My father's car was missing. I parked my car, jumped out, and screamed, "Mom!" as I ran to the door. I beat on my parents' door until my mom opened the door.

"Alexis?" She looked at me, alarmed.

I threw myself into her arms, sobbing, before I could even get in the house.

"Sweetie, what is it?" She held on to me and guided me into the living room. We sat on the couch. I took a deep breath and looked up at the ceiling.

"Honey. Do I need to call your father?"

I covered my face with my hands and sobbed.

"You are worrying me. What's wrong?"

I continued to shake my head, unable to get the words out. She walked out of the living room and, a minute later, came back with a glass of ice water. "Here," she ordered. "Drink this and calm down so you can explain to me what the hell is going on, baby."

Her phone rattled on the table next to me. "It must be that fool again. Someone is crank calling me. They been doing it all week. As much as I love your father, I wonder if he decided to finally fool around on me. He had better not."

I obeyed my mother, sipping the cold water and taking a deep breath before proceeding. I didn't respond to what she said because my problems were far worse than hers, and I felt resentful she would even have the nerve to bring her issues up at a time like this.

She set her phone down. "Now that you are a little calmer, tell me what's wrong, baby?"

"Santana is . . ." I continued to sob as I talked and had to take another deep breath before finishing. "He is cheating on me."

My mother pulled her lips in and appeared to try to keep a neutral expression. It didn't last long as she went from neutral to disapproving.

"Well, Alexis, you have to understand that you don't really know that man. You have only been seeing him for two months. That is not enough time to really know if you can trust a person. My instinct and his behavior give me the impression that he is really, really bad news." Her eyes were wide in emphasis.

That's why I didn't want to tell her. I knew she would just sit here and slander Santana. Yes, he had cheated. But he was not bad news! He was a good guy prior to me catching him cheating. Don't get me wrong. I was disappointed in the cheating aspect. If she thought that made him a bad guy, cool. I could accept that because right now he was not on my honorable or favorite person's list. But my mom didn't like him prior to me telling her about the cheating. It was just the icing on the cake. But I thought it unfair to already have the cake!

"Mom. I know it has only been two months but I didn't purposely fall in love with him. It just happened. You can't control who you love. I love Santana."

"After only two months? You sound delusional!"

"Mom! It's like that song by Jazmine Sullivan called 'Excuse Me.' He makes me want to do all I can for him. I don't know, it just happened that way. He is who I love. Even now, after this—"

The sounds of glass being broken cut me off.

My mother and I jumped up and ran outside to see where it was coming from. Once outside, we both spied the girl I had caught Santana with. She had a bat and she was busting the windows out of my mother's car. Then she went to mine and busted out my front window.

"What in the fuck are you doing destroying my property?" my mother demanded, confused as to who she was.

She looked up, spied me, and dropped the bat. Without a moment's hesitation, she said, "Bitch. Catch my fade!" She rushed toward me and started throwing a series of punches. I tried to fight back but I wasn't very good at it and, in all honesty, she was whipping my ass.

My mother yelled, "Get the fuck off of my daughter!"

The girl grabbed me in a headlock and punched me three more times in my face, knocking me on the ground.

"That's it, got-dammit. I'm going to kick your ass!" My mom ran toward her.

She pulled something out of her back pocket. A gun. She pointed it at my mother. It caused my mother to stop and hold her hands up.

I rolled over on my knees and when I looked toward her car, I saw Santana in her front seat.

It made my heart crumble. He had to be the one to tell her where my mother stayed. Why would he? How could he set me up like this?

"Stay the fuck back, old bitch! Call the police. I will have my homeboys come shoot this house up!" She glanced at me looking at Santana and laughed. "Yeah, you dumb bitch. You thought you was going to be able to fuck up my living situation for my kids and get away with it? I may get evicted now 'cause you busted out that window."

I closed my eyes briefly.

"You wanted to know if I was fucking him.

Now you know. And every time I see your ass, you going to catch my fade just of GP. So be ready."

She grabbed her bat off the ground. She then busted the back window of my mother's car.

I heard my mother make an angry sound in her throat. It was probably at the fact that she couldn't do anything because the girl had a gun.

I had a knot on my head and my bottom lip was busted from her attack. But more than that, my feelings were hurt that Santana was right there and didn't stop her from attacking me.

"I can't believe this shit!" my mother yelled as she drove away. "I'm calling the police and your father! That bastard was right in the front seat with that bitch! You better not have anything else to do with him, Alexis. I'm serious!"

Chapter 9

It had been a week since the crazy fiasco with the girl. I stopped talking to Santana. I tried to take my mother's advice and put the pain in God's hands, and hopefully He would wash it away. But my heart was heavy. So heavy.

My mother and I had wanted to file a police report against that girl but feared she would retaliate so we decided not to. Since the ordeal, I hadn't heard from Santana either. It bothered me but I knew the best thing to do was to try to get over him so he didn't have the chance to hurt me again. It sucked because I really thought we had something special. A couple times, I did want to call or text Santana. But I didn't and it took a lot for me not to. It hurt more that he didn't attempt to call or text me. Maybe he never did care about me. Maybe it was all me attaching myself to him. That's how it appeared because he sure as hell wasn't fighting to get me back. Maybe he loved the other girl. That hurt a lot, maybe even more than the actuality that he was cheating on me. Not to mention my mother was furious about the damage to our cars. Good thing we both had insurance and it was taken care of. But my heart wasn't.

I came to Bible Study and choir practice a hot mess. Before I could even get inside my dad stopped me.

"Alexis. I need to talk to you."

"Dad," I whined. "If this is about Mom's car I'm sorry. But we both have insurance so don't worry—"

"It's not about that. Although that is disappointing to hear that he had unfinished business that affected your family." He looked like he wanted to say more about Santana but he stopped, took a deep breath, and lowered his voice. I wondered why he used a filter when my mother sure as hell didn't. The day that crazy girl messed up my mother's car, she yelled and cursed for well over an hour after Santana and the girl left, all while I stared blankly out into space. "Alexis! If you have anything else to do with him . . ." she'd yelled.

I wondered why my dad didn't say the same. Maybe he didn't think Santana was all that bad. They had, after all, met each other first. Maybe he saw the good in Santana that my hurt and anger wouldn't let me see at that moment.

My dad interrupted my thoughts. "I need to speak to you about something else. Alexis, what's this I hear about you cursing at Marisol?"

That crybaby bitch. I pulled my shades over my red eyes. "Daddy. I have been through a lot this week. Now is not the time to talk about Marisol."

"Well, baby, I wish I could think about it like that but I can't. You work for me. So when it comes to business, I can't worry about your emotions and your breakup with Santana or any other boyfriend you end up with. Now, I can always fire you and then you can cry on my shoulder anytime, baby. But when it comes to work that's where my focus has to be. And it should be no-nonsense when it comes to that."

"Dad," I whined. "How can you talk to me that way?" I was hurt that he would even mention firing me.

"I need you to listen," he said sternly. "You don't speak to my employees that way. Marisol had been working for us for over ten years. If you are having issues where you can't control the way you talk to people, you need to take your ass home for the day until you can cool off and be the professional young lady I know you are."

I frowned and looked down at my heels.

"Do you understand what I'm telling you, baby?"

"Yes, Daddy. I do. I'm sorry. I didn't mean to offend Marisol."

"Okay. I expect you to apologize to her."

"Yes, Daddy. I will."

He gave me a hug and kissed me on my cheek. "Come on, baby. Let's go inside."

I followed my daddy, who had an arm around my shoulders.

When we went into the church, my dad went off to use the restroom. I took a seat in the last row, not really wanting to be bothered, even though there was still plenty of space up front as a lot of the members who attended Bible Study and choir practice hadn't made it there yet. But for the ones who were there, it was like there was an elephant in the room: awkward.

Sister Patterson took one look at me and said, "Alexis, baby. What you doing in the back? You know we always fill in the front rows. Come on, baby."

My bitch sister looked back at me and said, "Let her stay back there."

I got up and obeyed Sister Patterson and told my sister, "Don't start." Looking around at who else was there, I saw my mother hadn't made it there yet. She was probably still in traffic.

"All right, everyone, we'll get started in a few minutes. We're sure some members are in that five o'clock traffic. Let's just pray they make it here safely."

Sister Patterson led us into prayer. And I knew this sounded bad but my mind was on Santana. I wondered what he was doing and who he was doing whatever he was doing with. I wondered if it was that sicko who attacked me. But I strongly willed myself to focus on prayer. *Better he cheat on her than me.*

Pastor Owens waited another ten minutes and he started Bible Study.

"Today I'm going to talk about learning to discern. Ideally we should let God lead us in our decisions and work in our lives. When you turn away from this, you turn away what is better for you."

"Amen!" my sister shouted, a little too enthusiastically. I ignored her and tried to focus on what the pastor was saying.

"Galatians 2:20–21 says 'I will live by faith in the Son of God.' What this means is that because God loves you, He wants you to succeed. He will offer you continuous guidance and love as you have your journey. But the thing is, you have to accept that guidance. Part of accepting that guidance is making good decisions that the Lord is in favor of. The Lord is favorable of any decision that will help you flourish. Satan tricks us a lot by putting people in our lives who have no business being there. Someone who is a misrepresentation of us, with their own selfish plans, no matter how good they appear to be.

"*Well.*" That was my sister again.

I rolled my eyes.

As the Pastor continued to talk, I zoned out because I could not stop thinking about Santana. And when I tried to focus again, my sister made another snide-ass comment.

"Pastor. Someone needed to hear this. That's for sure!"

I had enough of her ass. "Shut the fuck up!" I yelled. When I realized I had cursed in church, I put a hand over my mouth and looked at my pastor apologetically. I was glad there were only a few people there. Still, the older ones looked at me and shook their heads.

My sister simply stared me down disdainfully.

"I'm the older sister. Pease show me some respect and stop taking jabs at me. I mean we can toss around dog bones if you like," I warned, "but I wonder what everyone would think of your skeletons!" I meant her failing her classes and just how wild and freaky she was getting in her dorm with girls and guys.

"Speak on it!" she challenged.

"Girls!" It was Sister Patterson.

Our pastor intervened. "Ladies, you two need to stop it. And be more respectful. It's not Sunday but we're still in church. We're still in worship."

"Yes, Pastor," we both chorused.

My father walked into the room and when my sister saw him she looked down at her Bible in her hand. I stood and walked off toward the exit. I didn't want a scene in church but my sister was a bitch who liked to push my buttons. Just then, Arianna walked into the church. She was a third grade schoolteacher and normally stayed to grade papers when school was over.

I walked up to Arianna and gave her a hug.

"How you holding up?" she asked me, concerned. These past few days, she had seen me cry and cry and cry over the situation with Santana. I was glad I had her support now. I just wished I had had it when I was actually with Santana. But it seemed they all sincerely felt I didn't belong with him. And truthfully, because of the cheating, I didn't feel I needed to be with him either.

"I would be okay if my bitch of a sister would leave me alone."

"You know she is childish."

"I have embarrassed myself far too much tonight. Just text me the songs we're singing on Sunday and I'll practice at home."

"Okay. And you know with report cards being done and tomorrow being Friday we really should go out, get your mind off of him and your immature sister. Let's make it an all-day thing. Go to Burke Williams, get some sushi, and then hit the club. Find you a new beau. What do you say?"

I knew the only way I would get over Santana was if I kept myself occupied. Not sit at home and cry and whine over him. That would keep my emotions right where they were. Moving on was the best thing. "Okay."

She gave me another hug. "And since you're here, you might as well stay. You know no choir rehearsal is the same without that powerhouse of a voice that you have."

I smiled.

"Come on."

Hand in hand, we walked back in like the best friends we were.

Chapter 10

True to my word, I kept my date with Arianna. We went to Glen Ivy Spa instead of Burke Williams, both got massages, skin resurfacing facials, manis and pedis. We had a blast. We went to eat at Katsu-ya and finished our night at the Century Club as planned.

"I'm so glad you decided to get over that loser and move on. Lord knows you can do so much better than him. You are young, pretty, and educated. You can have any man you want. You were, after all, engaged to a soon-to-be doctor. Trust that you are as special as you are. So don't be second-guessing a damn thing."

I got a text on my phone. I opened it and was surprised to see Santana had texted me. It made my heart beat faster. With extreme curiosity I read the text. It said simply:

Where you at?

I ignored it. A few seconds later, I got another one:

Respond.

So I did:

Out with a friend. Why do you care?

My friend continued to babble as I texted him back and forth.

Where? was his text.

Century Club. But it's none of your business! Cheater!

Go home, was his response.

No.

You need to bounce now or I'm coming up there.

"Who are you texting?" she demanded.

When I didn't answer because I didn't know how to respond to his text, she snatched my phone from me. "Him?" She instantly started typing something on my phone.

"What are you doing? I demanded, trying to snatch my phone.

"What you should be strong enough to do."

"Give me my phone back," I ordered, worried about what she texted to Santana.

She pushed me back when I reached for it and texted a couple more letters before handing it back to me.

I read the text she sent to Santana: Fuck off, loser. I'm on to bigger things.

"Why did you send him that?"

"Why didn't you? Why did you tell him where you were? It's like you want him back or something."

I did. Yes, he had lied to me. But that didn't stop me from wanting to be with him. Love doesn't die because of lies. It stays. And now I knew he obviously had some love for me, because of the texts. If I explained this to my friend she would just judge. She wouldn't get it. Just because she dropped her man for cheating, she thought I was weak if I didn't follow what she did.

"You didn't have to do that. I know how to speak for myself."

"Do you?" She narrowed her eyes at me and sipped her Adios.

"Whatever. I don't need to—"

I got another text: Will do. Take care.

Part of me wanted to tell him that wasn't my text, but another part of me felt it was for the best.

Arianna reaffirmed that when she said, "Him out of your life is for the best. After that crazy girl! Only a fool would continue to mess with that loser. We are queens and that is how we should be treated. Men should never half step when it comes to us."

These were all the words that came from our mothers. I had heard it a thousand times. Arianna came from a family just as successful as my family. Her mom was a lawyer and her father did cinematography for movies. Still, I didn't think I was as much of a snob as she was. I knew she was right but I didn't want to hear it. A part of me would always feel that Santana was different despite his cheating.

I tried to tune her out and downed my drink, an Adios as well. Once I felt a super buzz, Arianna pulled me out to the dance floor. The cut by Nicki Minaj and Rick Ross called "You The Boss" came on.

We were both dancing with two guys on the floor. Arianna was completely into it, whereas I was only halfway enjoying myself. But the liquor set in more and more and I found myself grinding against the guy and really enjoying it.

Then, as his hands rubbed up and down my curves, I felt someone yank my arm. I looked up into the menacing face of Santana. He gripped my left arm and pulled me off the dance floor, toward the bar. I didn't fight him. Once over to the bar, I set my glass on the counter.

"I thought I told you to get the fuck up out of here."

He had cheated on me and now he thought he could command me to do things? "Who are you to tell me what to do?" I demanded saucily.

"Your fucking nigga."

Suddenly Arianna emerged from the dance floor and over to us. She looked at Santana like he was shit. "Alexis, are you okay?"

"Get the fuck out of here. This my bitch. You act like you fucking her."

"Excuse me?" Her eyes were wide. "First off, my friend is no bitch." She put a finger in his face "*You* do not refer to her in that way." She said it like she was talking to her third grade students in her classroom. "Secondly, what you just implied is disgusting. We are best friends."

Santana glared at her and before she could say anything else, he grabbed my drink and flung it in her face.

I gasped at the same time as my friend. She instantly started crying. "You bastard!"

"Yeah, bitch!" He grabbed my arm again and pulled me out of the club. I glanced back at my friend, who stood in the same spot, still crying.

He pulled me all the way to the parking lot. I tried to snatch away from him but he said, "Girl, don't play with me."

I relaxed my body. He stopped in front of his car.

"Why are you here?" I asked.

"Fuck you mean why am I here? And tell that bitch friend of yours to stay the fuck out of my business."

I shouldn't have liked when he started cursing and got aggressive, but I did. Still I said, "You said 'take care' as if we were done."

"We ain't never done. Understand?"

"How do you get to make that determination when you lied to me and cheated on me?" I was now crying.

"Man." He shook his head. "You talking? You were still actively fucking your fiancé and still with him after I told you to leave him alone! It took for him to commit suicide for you to be done and now you on me, church girl? And real talk, that bitch don't mean nothing to me. You have my heart. Like no one has ever had."

"Then why?"

He took a deep breath. "Look, man. You really wanna know the truth?"

"Yes," I said quickly, scared he would change his mind and not tell me. I desperately wanted to know the truth.

"That ho was someone I used to fuck with long before I knew you. I didn't know we were going to get close like we did. I started fucking with her again on some necessity type of shit. I needed somewhere to lay my head. I can't stay at that pad no more. They gave us all thirty days' notice 'cause they tearing that place down. When I brought up moving in with you and you holding me down, you wasn't with that. You spoke on marriage first, saying I needed to put a ring on it. And that's cool. And while I'm crazy as hell for you, to keep it gravy, baby, it is soon for us to be speaking on marriage. I'm not established yet and in no position to put a ring on your finger. All those things will happen but not right now. I want to give you the world and one day, trust on my life, I will. But we're dating right now. I mean what could I give you if we married? I'm still trying to finish school, get a good job to hold you down. But you want a ring now. Come on, baby, it wouldn't be smart. But ol' girl. She was waiting for me to move in. That's what that shit was about. She need someone to be around her kids and someone to warm her bed. I needed a crib to rest my head. Not no emotional feelings type of shit you thinking of." He repeated, "You got my heart."

So really this was my fault. If I had let him move in with me, we wouldn't be in this situation. How much more could I possibly fuck up? Here was a man who needed me and I almost lost him to another woman because of my stupidity. Although he had explained things thoroughly, still I pressed the issue.

I took a deep breath. "So this wasn't about her being a better woman than me and you loving her more?"

"You made it about that because she was willing to hold it down for me in a way you wasn't. Like that song that was playing while you was grinding on that nigga said . . ." He gripped my waist and said, "Which I better not ever see happen again . . . What that song say?"

I cleared my throat and recited the line from Nicki Minaj's lyrics. "'I'll do anything you say, 'cause you the boss.'"

"Yeah. Too bad you don't feel that way. But that's how it's supposed to be. That is even in the Bible. Man is designed to lead if he a real man. And that's me. I'm a real nigga all day. Not like any of these square-ass niggas in that bullshit-ass club. And I'm telling you that I love you, want you, but if you can't hold it down for me don't expect another bitch not to be willing to and not able to take your spot in my heart."

I didn't want any of that to happen. I loved him already and I didn't want to compete with another bitch. So if I could fulfill every single need he had to the best of my abilities, how could anyone else come and take Santana from me?

"Come over and fuck me real good, and in the morning, make your decision, baby, just make it the right one. You drove?"

The thought of making love to him caused a jolt to my lower body.

"No. My friend did."

"Then leave that bitch here and come on and take care of your daddy. This dick has been missing you all week."

Chapter 11

I decided to take Santana back. When we left the club that night and I went to his house I made love to him all night long. We woke up and made love three more times. Then we had lunch at Ruth's Chris. Santana was getting hooked on that place. Over lunch, we had decided that it was best if he moved in with me. I wasn't going to have to run the risk of damn near losing him again because he had a bad living situation that I could have easily fixed.

I took a deep breath and looked at Santana nervously as we were parked outside of the girl Reina's house. "I really don't feel comfortable doing this." Santana wanted me to go inside and pack up the rest of his things.

"I told you it would be okay. I already talked to her ass."

"Well, why can't you do it?"

"I told you. I don't want to see her kids. They had gotten attached to me and I had gotten attached to them. It will be hard to see them. She agrees."

"But I don't want any problems with her."

"I told you that girl is done tripping off you. She accepts that she not in your league and she lost me to you. Watch. I'll call her right now."

I waited, almost not breathing as he dialed her number and put her on speaker phone.

"Hello?" She sounded calm, so that was good.

"Hey. My girl is going to come in here and get my shit. You not going to fuck with her are you?"

"I'm too grown for that shit. The only reason why I did that is because she disrespected where I lie with my kids. You paid for the window to get fixed and I didn't get evicted. I'm Gucci. I'm good. I'm telling you. Besides my kids are here. I don't be doing all that shit in front of them. She good."

"Cool." He ended the call. "Go on."

I took a deep breath and opened the car door. I walked on shaking legs up to her house. I reassured myself that I would be okay. She seemed fine and I wondered if I would be that calm if I were her. Since I wasn't a fighter, if she were in my shoes, I would probably just let her get his stuff, only because I couldn't fight. But if I could fight I would want to fight for the man I loved. But according to Santana, their situation was never a love thing. He had said that I had his heart.

Before I even had a chance to knock, she opened the door with a smile. "You good. Come on."

"Thank you." I stepped inside and followed her. Up close, I saw she was a very pretty girl with a gigantic booty. "He really don't have a lot of stuff. It's in the room on the bed. I'll get you some trash bags to put it in."

There were several pairs of tennis shoes on the bed along with some jeans and a few shirts. There was also an Xbox 360 and a Wii.

She came back and handed me two black trash bags. "Here you go. And make sure there is nothing else in the closet that I may have missed."

"Thank you."

I quickly put the items in one of trash bags. Then I slipped his games into the other bag. I still didn't like this bitch. For one she had been with my man while I was with him. And for two, she had messed up my mother's car and my car. But I appreciated the fact that she was going to move on from Santana and not cause us any more problems.

I looked in her closet and saw nothing else that appeared to belong to Santana.

"That was easy," I mumbled to myself.

I grabbed the bags and walked out of her bedroom. When I made it past the hallway, toward the living room, I jumped because there were now two more girls in the house. They were all seated on the couch. The aroma of weed was now in the room. The two girls smiled at me and said, "Hello."

Across from them was a cute little boy who looked like he was about seven, and a little girl who looked to be around four. Reina was combing the little girl's hair.

"Hi." I gave a nervous smile and proceeded to walk past them. I closed the space between me and the door with quick steps; my heart started beating at a rapid rate.

I grabbed the doorknob and, before I could turn it, I felt the pressure of a fist slam into the back of my head. My head instantly hit the door, making me so dizzy that I dropped to the floor; the bags fell from my hands.

I was then rushed by all three women.

"You dumb bitch! You thought you were just going to come in here and be able to walk out?"

All three women started throwing punches. That wasn't the worst. The little boy started kicking me in my head.

I hid my head in my forearms, blocking some of the kicks. I screamed like I was running through a hail of bullets as they continued to attack me. I stood and grabbed the doorknob but the hits never stopped coming. I still managed to get away from them and find the strength to run out of the door, screaming for my life.

I ran to the car and opened the passenger's side door. I glanced back and saw them all coming after me and laughing.

I jumped into the car and before I could close the door, one of the chicks grabbed my hair while Reina pummeled me in my head, saying, "Yeah, bitch, catch my fade again! Go to the police this time. I know where the fuck your mama live. We will fuck her up too! Mess up that pretty-ass house, *groove*." The other girl was kicking the shit out of my car.

Santana looked surprised. "What the fuck?" Santana leaned over me and shoved Reina back and told the other girl, "Let go of her fucking hair!"

I screamed for my life.

She finally let me go and I closed the door. Santana pulled off but they still chased after us.

I hid my head in my shoulder and cried all while Santana said, "We done. We don't ever have to worry about them crazy bitches again. But, babe, where is my stuff?"

"I . . ." I was breathing hard and couldn't talk.

"Breathe, baby," he said as he steered the car.

"I left it."

"What? You left my shit?"

"Yes! We can't ever go back there. They are crazy. Whatever I left, I will replace. Tomorrow."

My head was pounding and I knew I had to look a mess with more knots on my forehead, a black eye, and my hair all wild. I wanted to go to the police but I thought about what they said. I didn't want my mother in any more drama. She already hated Santana and would probably blame him. The best thing to do was to put this whole experience behind me. I smoothed my hair back from my face, hoping the experience didn't give me posttraumatic stress disorder. All I wanted him to do was get me home.

Chapter 12

My friend stood in front of the door with a shocked look on her face as Santana and I moved his things into the house she and I shared together.

"Alexis! What happened to your face? Did he hit you?"

Santana started laughing.

"No. I got attacked. I don't want to discuss it." My head was killing me from the beating I just got. It was like I was moving hell and earth for this man. But that's how much I wanted him.

She narrowed her eyes at me. "What are you doing with those bags and suitcases?"

"What does it look like?"

"It looks like you're moving him into *our* house. But the reason why I am asking what you are doing is because I would think that, this being our house, you would have consulted me first!"

"It's my father's house. So that makes it mine and never made it yours."

She looked baffled by my comment. "So you are moving him in here and you never thought to let me know or thought to even ask me if I would be okay with it, when you know it would positively piss me off?"

Santana didn't respond. He just started putting his suitcases in my bedroom. He came back out and grabbed two more. Arianna and I were standing near the hallway now. He bumped her with his suitcase and she scowled at him.

"Before you go off on him, he didn't do that on purpose," I said quickly.

But it seemed she was far too lost in the situation to even care that he had bumped her. She just stared at him. "We have been best friends since preschool. We did everything together. I can't believe you are choosing him: a man who has clearly shown you that he is no good for you. And still you are choosing him over me."

"I'm not. I love you. I will always be your friend. I'm not turning my back on you as a friend, Arianna. You mustn't say things like that. We have far too much history for me to ever think of doing anything like that. I don't ever want to stop being your friend. Why can't we all live in this house together? He's going to share a room with me."

"Because—"

Santana walked past, not bothering to say anything to my friend, and told me, "I'm going to get me some smokes. I'll be right back."

He kissed me while eying Arianna. She looked away, disgusted.

When he left, she turned back to me and said, "He makes my skin crawl. Alexis, I hate him for you. He is garbage and he will only bring you down. I see it. He is bad news. Why can't you see that?" There were tears in her eyes. She looked so concerned.

"You have him all wrong. Santana is a little rough around the edges but he is not a bad guy. And he loves me."

"Are you insane? This is the same man who cheated on you!"

"That was my fault. If I had let him move in he wouldn't have done that. And he's done with her. I'm not a saint. Remember I was juggling him and Dannon for a whole month!"

"It's like he's got you brainwashed. I don't know who you are anymore. And I'm really afraid for you."

"You just can't see past being privileged to give anyone a chance. Did you know that Phaedra from *The Real Housewives of Atlanta*'s husband has a record? I was reading about it on Mediatakeout.com. She said that us black women are creating genocide by not dating men because they aren't on our financial level or that have a criminal record."

She seemed to have tuned me out. "No man ever throws a drink in a woman's face or calls her a bitch. My daddy has never treated my mom that way, nor has any man ever treated me that way, nor will I allow it. If a man even raises his voice at me the wrong way I'm gone. I know what I am worthy of and I thought you did too. Your mother and father raised you better. You're a fool. If he moves in here, I'm moving out . . . today. I will call my daddy right now. And if that piece of shit ever comes near me again, he will be in jail. You have a decision to make so you better make it now."

I swallowed hard. I didn't want my friend to move out. I also didn't want her to be mad at me or feel like I was choosing Santana over her. Why was she being so selfish? Why couldn't she just accept Santana? If she was really my best friend and loved me like she always said she did, she would. She had no real reasons to dislike him other than the fact that he threw a drink in her face. But she needed to get over that and understand that she played a part in it. I wasn't saying he was right for doing that and I told him he was wrong. But she gave him so much attitude that night, what did she expect?

I cleared my throat and said, "He's staying."

At those words she closed her eyes and kept them closed. She looked really hurt.

I touched her on her shoulder. "But I want—"

She opened her eyes and snatched away from me. She pulled out her iPhone and made a phone call. "Daddy! I'm coming home now. I need you to send a mover to get my things. No. I haven't packed and I'll tell you why later. I'm coming home now."

She grabbed her purse and walked out, not even bothering to say goodbye to me.

Although I missed my friend, I enjoyed playing wifey to Santana. He was still in school and I was still working for my daddy. I would come home, cook, and serve him. In return, he would give me the best lovemaking I had ever experienced. It felt good to be able go to sleep with him and wake up next to him. I wanted to please him in any way that I possibly could. True to my word, the next day after all that drama, I took my credit card and replaced all the items I had left at that psychotic bitch's house. And she had left us alone. There were no more phone calls from her and she hadn't come to my mother's house again, either. Speaking of my mother, she was very angry at the fact that I had not left Santana alone. She was even angrier at the fact that we were now living together. But there was nothing she could do about it but accept it.

My daddy seemed indifferent to the whole situation. He really wasn't tripping off of Santana. He did have a long talk with Santana and told him he didn't like the girl coming over to his house and that he expected Santana to handle it. Santana said he would and none of us would have to worry about the girl again. Matter of fact, Santana and my father had even gone out for drinks a couple times. I was happy to know my daddy was being open-minded. It was a lost cause with my mother. She never wanted to hear anything about Santana, unless it was that I was leaving him.

And, as for my friend, it had been two months since I had heard from her. She also wouldn't return my calls. And when she saw me in church, she wouldn't even acknowledge I was there. It hurt. I felt like she should have been more mature about the situation. If she wanted to throw away a twenty-year friendship then that was her fucking loss. Santana was here to stay.

I sang my heart out to Jazmine Sullivan as her song, "Excuse Me," blasted from my iPod in my car. I could hit the same high-pitched notes she hit.

"'Excuse me if I'm sounding crazy but you've been the one I've been hoping and waiting for.'" I turned down the street to my house. I parked in my driveway, got out, and grabbed my purse, attaché case, and the bag from Outback Steakhouse. It was late and I had no real energy to cook today. I simply wanted to make love to Santana and rest up.

I came through the door and looked for Santana. When I didn't see him in the living room, I set my purse and attaché case on the couch. I walked into the dining room and set the bag from Outback down on the dining room table. "Babe. Where are you?"

I walked into our bedroom and found him in bed, watching the news.

I smiled and slipped off my shoes, crawling on the bed toward him. "Hey, baby." I lay on his chest and kissed him. "I got us some pasta and crab legs from Outback for dinner."

"Okay. Rest with me for a little while." He gripped his arms around my waist and held me close to him. See, this was the Santana other people didn't get to see. He had an incredible soft and gentle side. Some days he simply wanted to rest in my arms and he wanted me to rub his back. He said it comforted him and made him feel loved because he never really felt loved until he met me. I got it, even while others didn't: the ones who made him out to be a bad person. But they based it on the wrong things. They looked at his past and the fact that he didn't have a degree or a job making a lot of money. Why did these things automatically label him a bad guy? So when he met people like this, you damn right he gave them nothing but an attitude. That was because his perspective was simple: "If you want to judge me before getting to know me then why the fuck should I show you all the good in me? Like my man Jay-Z said, 'Middle finger in the air, nigga gripping my balls.'"

But that was fine. *Let all his sweetness be reserved for me.*

I closed my eyes and enjoyed his embrace. I started humming softly in his ear.

"What are you singing, baby?" he asked, stroking his hands up and down my back.

"Jazmine Sullivan's 'Excuse Me.' Love that song."

There was a nice breeze blowing in the room and it felt so good being in his arms. It made me feel loved. It reminded me how much I loved, desired, and wanted him.

"Why do you love it?" he asked in a husky voice.

"Because she feels so passionate about a guy. Her love for him makes her want to do whatever she can to make him happy . . . And that's how I feel about you."

"Oh yeah?" He rubbed on my butt.

"Yes. What I am telling you is one hundred percent sincere. I love you, Santana. You are like my drug and I will do whatever I can to keep you happy. Being in your presence makes me happy. Each day I care about you more. It's to a capacity that is almost scary for me because I have never felt this."

"Hmmm," was what he said, low in his throat. He kissed me on my neck. "Sing that song to me. I wanna hear it."

I closed my eyes and started singing softly. I knew my pitch was perfect from years of singing in the choir at church, and in classes I had taken at school. My singing had been known to make people cry.

"I closed my eyes and belted out:
And just to see you smiling at me
Baby, you don't even have to ask me
Don't care what the task be, if it makes
you happy . . ."

I continued to sing as Santana softly rolled me on to my back so he was free to slip his body between my legs. It threw off my concentration when he pulled off my slacks and underwear. He then started going down on me, causing me to moan.

"Keep singing," he ordered, teasing my clit with his tongue.

But now it was hard for me to keep up with the words of the song because he was making me feel so good. So I went to humming it. He laughed and continued to pleasure me.

"Santana. Damn." My eyes closed as I savored the pleasure. My hands sunk in his curly hair. It didn't stop him from letting up. In fact, he got more into it, sticking fingers in me while he continued to suck on my clit.

"Sing," he ordered. "Or I'm going to stop."

"'Because no one, no not no one ever made me feel like I could be dreaming 'cause you can't be—'"

I didn't stop because of the pleasure. I stopped this time because I felt a presence in the room and, sure enough, when I opened my eyes, I saw the older Jamaican man I had seen before in Santana's pad walk into our bedroom.

I gently kicked Santana in the chest and quickly covered up with my blanket.

"Damn, baby, what?"

He looked behind him and jumped at the figure. "Aye, man! What the fuck?" He stood and looked at the dude again. When he recognized who it was, he lowered his voice. "Dylan. Man, what you doing in my girl's crib?"

"No call? Move and say nothing to me? Me panicked and had to check up on chu."

I wondered what he was talking about and if Santana was involved in some mess with this man. He had a lot of nerve just walking in my home without knocking. I watched Santana and tried to read his face for a sign of what the hell was going on.

Santana wiped his face with his hands, all while Dylan stared me down and sucked on one of his teeth in the corner of his mouth, like he had a piece of meat stuck in it. I looked away.

"Come on, man, let's go for a walk." He walked toward the door, paused, and looked over his shoulder at me. "Alexis. I'll be back."

"Is everything okay?"

"Maybe. Maybe no. Me be outside," the Jamaican man said before walking out the door.

"Santana."

He put a hand up at me. "Stop. I told you about that." He slipped out of the bedroom and closed the door behind him.

I closed my mouth and swallowed up the last of my sentence, in which I was going to question him on who this man was. I felt his business with Santana was something illegal, like drugs. I wondered if Santana was selling them for this man. What else could it be? The man seemed like a crook. He seemed like bad news. I would have to find a way to get Santana to tell me who he was and why he was now popping up at my house. I wondered if Santana had given him my address.

I got up and slipped into the shower. I did this so I could keep myself engaged in something until he came back. Once out of the shower, I dried off and slipped on a nightgown. I went into the kitchen and warmed up the dinner. I placed two plates on the table and set the two platters of fettuccine Alfredo and king crab legs in the middle. I pulled out a bottle of merlot and a bottle of Hennessy. Sometimes, during dinner, Santana liked to sip on Hennessy.

Chapter 13

A whole hour had passed and Santana had not come back. I ate a little of the food and patiently waited. When two more hours passed, I called Santana's cell. He wouldn't pick up. When I caught myself stressing, I reminded myself that I was a woman of faith. I didn't worry. My mother had always taught me that. I stayed up and watched TV. When my eyes got too heavy, I ended up dozing off on the couch.

When I felt someone carrying me into the bedroom, I opened my eyes and saw Santana looking down at me.

I moaned and stretched in his arms. "Baby. What happened? Where you been? What did he want with you? Are you in trouble?"

He carried me into the room and laid me on the bed. Then he sat next to me. "Damn! Which one do you want me to answer? You know I'm a private-ass nigga and I don't involve you in my personal business. Yet you still question me."

"Well, he came to my home so it makes the situation a little different don't you think?" I tried to keep any type of attitude out of my voice because I knew he didn't like that.

"That shit won't happen again. Trust. He just a nigga from my old neighborhood and he needs some soldiers to put in some work for him. At first, with the situation of me needing a place to stay, I was on it. That's why they were there that day you just popped up at my crib. But when we moved in together, I decided I wanted to do right by you. So I got back at him and I told him no. I wanted any illegal activity to be a part of my past. I'm almost thirty years old. I guess he came back around and propositioned me again because he knows I'm a good and loyal solider. But I turned him down again. All that shit he was talking was just that. Talk. He ain't gonna do shit."

I knew by "soldiers" and "putting in work," whatever the Jamaican man wanted him to do had to be something illegal. Maybe drugs or guns. And I knew I should just accept what he told me and leave it alone but I asked anyway, "Soldiers for what?"

He scowled at me. "Here you go. It won't stop with the questions! I'm not telling you no more information. Just know he won't be coming here anymore." He slapped me on my ass. "Get up and make me something to eat."

I jumped from the bed and rushed into the kitchen. He followed me. I didn't want to make him angry so I was quiet for a minute as I warmed up the leftover food from Outback.

I served him the pasta and crab legs, sat across from him and watched him eat. He ate the food with a massive frown on his face. There was awkward silence.

"Man. Take your ass to sleep!" he snapped in an irritated voice.

I got up from the table, did as he ordered. I didn't want to piss him off any further.

The last thing I was trying to do was pry. I just couldn't help but be curious about the guy. But I should have just accepted what he said and left it at that. I was also glad he had done the right thing and turned him down.

A few minutes later, Santana came into the room. He belched and closed the door.

I turned my head on my pillow and watched him pull off his boxers and get in the bed. I turned back on my side. I soon felt his hands shove my nightgown up and rub on my bare bottom.

I kept silent as he lifted one of my legs in the air. His hardness pressed against my thigh. He stuffed it into my pussy. I wasn't wet. I was super tight and dry but as soon as his ten inches completely filled me, my walls loosened up and I became super slick with cream. I moaned as he pumped in a rough manner.

"Stay the fuck out of my business. You hear me, girl?" He jabbed me roughly.

"Okay, baby. Sorry."

He gripped my hips and slammed in and out of me.

I cried out loudly.

"Who the fuck is your nigga?"

"You are, baby!"

He was putting it on me. Dicking me down majorly.

"Then let me handle shit. And stop fucking questioning me!" He pulled his dick all the way out, making me protest. "You want this dick back in you, huh?"

I moaned as the head of his dick slipped back into me.

He tossed me aside, got up, and yanked me off the bed by one of my hands. Next thing I knew, Santana had me standing with my legs shoulder length apart and holding on to the walls. He jabbed and jabbed me in my pussy. Nut was literally leaking down my inner thighs.

"You fucking with a real nigga now." He continued to fuck the shit out of me, sticking a finger in my asshole as he continued to go inside of me.

It was all I could take. I screamed, losing all the strength in my body. Unable to stand, I slid to the ground, cumming all over myself.

He started laughing. "I don't know if you can handle a nigga like me." He tossed me on my back, spread my legs wide, and entered me again.

I didn't say anything because my body was still convulsing and he continued to fuck me, making me have orgasm after orgasm after orgasm. In all honesty, sometimes I didn't know if I could handle a man like him either. But I wanted him so bad that I was going to try my absolute best to keep him.

Chapter 14

Santana's anger melted away over the week-end and we went to church. Since I was going to sing another solo, I made sure I looked nice. I wore a real pretty dress. It was red, fuchsia, yellow, and blue. The print was floral and it bunched at the waist and billowed out to my knees. I wore a pair of Red Bottom fuchsia pumps. I also placed a few curls in my usually straight mane.

When I asked Santana how I looked, he said, "You know you a looker. I bet all them niggas on the congregation want to fuck you and they mad at me 'cause they can't."

I laughed, not because the joke was necessarily funny, but because he was no longer angry at me anymore for prying and he was now engaging with me.

Once we made it to the church doors, we walked inside, hand in hand. I dared anyone to say something to me about bringing him. In my opinion, some of the members of my church were nothing but hypocrites. What happened to, "Every saint has a past and every sinner has a future"?

As we walked inside the church that I had grown up in, I kept my head held high, proud to have Santana on my arm.

I glanced at my watch. We were early. The actual service hadn't started yet.

I ignored all the stares. The only one in the church who I knew wouldn't judge me was Justin. But he was still out of town. He had gone to meet with a producer in New York. I couldn't wait until he came back. Then I would at least have someone in the church to talk to. But then again maybe he would judge me just like everyone else.

Santana sat in the back pew. I started to ask him to sit with me next to my mother but I stopped myself. I knew neither of them would want to be near each other.

I blew him a kiss and walked up to my mother, who was seated in the front row. She was fiddling with her phone. I gave her a kiss on the cheek. "Hi, Mommy," I said cheerfully.

"Hi," she said dryly.

Not knowing what to say, I asked, "Is that weirdo still calling you?"

"Yes."

"Why don't you just change your number?"

"Because I have a lot of contacts and I'm not going to inconvenience myself or them because some sicko wants to play on a fifty-year-old woman's phone. Or better yet, someone your father is screwing."

I gave her a doubtful look. "Mom. Daddy is not doing that. After all these years why would he?"

"Because people change that's why. Just go with the choir," she ordered. I knew she wanted to say more but didn't want anyone in the church to hear . . . She didn't ask me about Santana. That bothered me. When I was with Dannon, she had always asked me how he was, baked him goodies, bought him gifts and whatnot. He was so spoiled. Yet, she still was refusing to accept Santana. It bothered me but I didn't want to argue. So I said, "All right, Mommy."

We usually started our worship service by singing a few selections. As I sang, Santana's eyes locked with mine and he didn't look away. It showed the power of the emotions between the two of us.

After our selection, the praise dancers performed. My sister was in the group of four girls. I watched Santana laugh at them and shake his head. I knew he was probably laughing at my sister. She was a little demon trying to resemble an angel, with her all-white long, flowing dress and bare feet.

Next was the pastor's sermon. Santana appeared to really be listening. It was Proverbs 3.

They did the offering, gave visitors the opportunity to become members, and then it was time for me to close out the service by singing my solo. I started singing "I Trust You." My mother instantly got teary-eyed. My father did as well. And even though my sister had been a bitch to me lately I could tell she equally admired my voice.

Before I finished, I saw one of the women sitting in the pews get up. She caught Santana's attention and he watched her sashay down the aisle. As I felt my jealously set in, I reminded myself that all men looked; it meant nothing. She had a big ass and I had a big ass, so what? If I was walking down the aisle and her man was sitting in the pew, he probably would look at me. So none of that bothered me. What bothered me was when she turned to him and slyly did a "come hither" with her index finger. And without a moment's hesitation, he got up and followed her out of the church. That bothered the hell out of me and made me switch my next four words, which were supposed to be "I Trust You Lord," to "fucking bitch!"

I received a chorus of gasps.

My sister laughed and shook her head at me while my mother and father both looked mortified.

I closed my eyes briefly and tried to go on with the song. That was a struggle for me. The whole time I was wondering where the hell he was going with that bitch. I had never even seen her in our church before. Still, I had to finish the song. I continued with the song, hoping that if I hit the high note (which I normally could) that would make them all forget that I just dropped the F and B bombs in church. I tried to concentrate on the words but all I saw were images of him and her. Maybe her sliding him her number, or maybe she was rubbing up against my man.

Fucking whore!

I wanted to kill her. I sped up the remaining words of the song. This left the band looking at me like I was crazy. I ignored them. With just three lines of the song left, I watched the doors of the church burst open and Santana run back inside.

The two Jamaican men I had seen at my house were chasing after him with guns drawn. Santana ran toward the stage. I dropped the microphone as they went after him. Once they caught him they started whipping on him.

I watched fearfully.

I heard more gasps and screams from members of the church. Santana was getting physically assaulted and there was nothing I could do about it. I screamed as one of them stomped Santana in his head. The brown-skinned one waved a gun at the entire church so everyone stood frozen and watched helplessly.

"Pussy clot!" the assaulter yelled and continued to whip on him.

My hand was over my mouth as Santana yelled out from the pain. Every time he yelled I screamed and begged them to stop.

I felt so helpless.

"Me want what's owed. Twenty-four hours, pussy clot."

He gave Santana one final punch and the man holding the gun kicked him in the face, making me cry out again. Then they walked out of the church.

Santana howled out in pain. "Babe!" he yelled.

"I'm here!" I rushed over to help Santana. "We need to get you to a hospital now."

"No. Fuck the hospital." He struggled to stand to his feet.

"Get him out of this church!" my mother yelled. "He is never welcome here again got-dammit!" She stormed off while the rest of the church watched us like we were a movie, our every move.

My father was kind enough to help me get Santana up and helped him outside to the car. "Santana, I really think you need to go to the hospital."

"No, baby, just . . . Let's go home. I'll be okay."

"Okay."

My dad was silent and simply helped him into the passenger's seat.

"Thanks, Daddy."

"All right," was all he said, not giving me eye contact.

I rushed over to the driver's side, got in, started the ignition, and drove us home.

Once we got home, I laid Santana on the couch. I cleaned his busted lip and bloody nose, and gave him some ice wrapped in a paper towel for the knots on his forehead. I also gave him two Motrin and a glass of water. As I did this, there were so many thoughts flying through my head. First off, who was the woman who beckoned him outside? Why did Santana go? Was he trying to get her number? And why the hell did those two men who he claimed simply wanted him to work for them attack him like that? There was a whole lot more to this story.

I needed to know what the hell was going on. I knew there was no real way to find out other than asking.

I took a deep breath. "Santana—"

"Look. Before you start, let me explain, baby. I wasn't one hundred percent honest with you." He struggled to sit up on the couch. Once he was in a sitting position, he coughed, grimaced, and grabbed at his ribcage. I figured it was hurting from all the kicking.

"I know I told you that they wanted me to put in some work for them and that I turned them down. The thing is, I did put in work for them."

"Santana! Was it drugs?"

"No. Just listen. They involved in white-collar shit. Credit cards. They sell the cards for three stacks a piece and the credit limit be like ten thousand. Them goat-breath muthafuckas fronted me a couple cards and I sold them shits in a few hours. Shit was crazy. It was better than dope money. So I bought some more cards. Hell, a nigga was on." He aimed a finger at me. "One thing you gotta always remember is niggas is always watching your shit. You think you on a come up and you really they next come up. Niggas ran up in my spot and robbed my ass. That was another reason I pressured you into letting me move in with you. I was trying to buy some time to get the money for those cards. I tried to explain the situation to Dylan but he didn't want to hear that shit." *Oh, Lord.* Santana was involved in white-collar crime. He had lied to me. And the fact that he held on to this secret all this time greatly disappointed me. Santana should have never gotten involved with those two men. Not to mention that he could have gotten a lot of time if he had gotten caught. Good thing he stopped after the robbery. Or did he? I was disappointed about the fact that Santana made it seem like his illegal activity was a part of his past.

"And who was the girl?" I demanded.

"I don't know that bitch. That was a setup for me to go outside. She obviously works for Dylan."

"If you didn't know her why did you go?"

"Man, you seriously asking me about another bitch at a time like this? Why would I try to get at a girl at your church? I went outside to smoke a cigarette. I didn't want to get up and cause no type of disruption so when that bitch went, I said fuck it and went. It could have been a nigga who went outside and I would have still went. If *she* was a nigga you wouldn't be asking me this."

I sighed, relieved that it wasn't what I thought it was. But there was still more worry because he did, after all, owe debt to two men who just beat the shit out of him.

"How much money do you owe them?"

"Twenty stacks."

Instantly my mind calculated how much money I had in my savings and how much I could get off my credit card. While I certainly could get some of the money he owed, I didn't have $20,000 at my disposal. Lord knows that I should have, but I had always been a shopaholic. This addiction had never been a problem for me before. Now it was. The only people I knew who had that amount of money at their disposal were my parents. But they weren't going to just give it to me without a very good explanation. Knowing my mom, who was so inquisitive, she probably would figure out who it was for right off the bat.

"Baby. Say something." He pleaded with his eyes. "I need you."

My eyes started to water because I felt so distressed. "What will happen if you don't pay them?"

"Them fucking Jamaicans are ruthless. You saw what they did to me inside of a church."

His next choice of words had my eyes wide and my stomach doing flip-flops.

"Them niggas are probably going to kill me."

Then Santana did something I had never seen him do before: he broke down crying and crawled toward me, burying his head in my lap. I held him and rubbed his back, never in my life feeling so needed by a person.

To comfort him I said, "Don't worry, baby. Calm down. I'm going to figure this out. I promise."

Chapter 15

The next morning I got up bright and early, went to the bank, and cleaned out my savings account. I only had $7,000 in it. I then got a cash advance on my Bank of America credit card. That brought my total to $11,000. I was still $9,000 short. Although my next course of action was a tough one, the images of those two vile men beating on my baby made me do it. I felt I essentially had no choice. I pulled out $9,000 from my father's account. Since my father owned a total of six apartment complexes, I chose the one that always had the highest balance: the one Marisol managed. It was a two-bedroom complex, located in Cerritos, California. Since it was a better neighborhood than the others, we charged $1,800 a month for the rent. I transferred the money from this account to my checking account. I then went to another branch to take the money out of my account. Although, to the bank, it probably wouldn't look suspicious because it was my account and my account was legit, I was just more comfortable going to a different branch.

I planned on paying my father back. I would simply put the money back little by little.

Once I was done, I shot back by to my office, thinking even slicker. I felt $9,000 was a big withdrawal even if that building brought in the most revenue. Each complex had its own account and only I had access to them. The managers were each responsible for bringing me the apartment's rent and the deposits. I got on my laptop and pulled out amounts from the accounts of my dad's other buildings and put them into the Cerritos complex's account. I pulled out smaller, staggered amounts, like $2,000 from one, $1,500 from one, $900 from another, and so on until I got to $9,000. I realized that was being a little paranoid and anal; the reason being that my father never kept track of this stuff because he trusted me to do it. But I just wanted to make sure it wasn't noticeable in case he did decide to check.

I honestly felt a little bad for taking money from him. But I reminded myself that I was going to put it back.

As I waited for the last transfer to process, I damn near jumped out of my seat when my father walked into my office.

"Dad." I eyed the screen as it continued to process.

"Hey, baby."

My dad rarely visited me at the office.

"I came to talk to you."

"Dad, can't it wait?" The transaction was taking a year and a day to be complete!

"No. It can't wait."

The screen said that my transaction was approved. I sighed, relieved, and gave him my full attention. "Go ahead, Daddy."

"Now, I have always been proud of you and all the hard work you have been doing these last couple years, since you finished college. But, lately, I have been getting a lot of complaints from the apartment managers. They say you're short with them and very snappy. Baby, they also said you are not being as efficient with their service and repair requests as you used to be. That is really disappointing to hear."

I closed my eyes briefly. My daddy was right. I wasn't at my best at work because my mind was always wrapped around Santana. My job had always been my top priority. And now my top priority had switched to Santana. All else was secondary. I couldn't tell my father this. I tried to think of a believable excuse.

"Well?" He stood in front of me with his arms crossed under his chest.

"Dad. I have had so much on my mind and you just don't understand that everything you ask me to do is very demanding. I'm really doing my best and it really hurts me that you don't see that. I am overseeing six different complexes. When your managers screw up, I'm here to fix it. Every time they request petty cash or money over five hundred dollars, I'm sorry, I'm not going to jump to give it to them, because I want to make sure the money is being spent properly and not wasted." I even dropped some crocodile tears for effect.

My dad seemed to be buying it and he even looked like he felt bad. "I'll tell you what. Since you feel that way, maybe the solution to this problem is to hire someone to help you out. Take some of the workload off of you. Someone who will be reliable and really assist you. "

The last thing I needed, especially since I had taken some funds from my father, was someone all in my mix. "Daddy. I really don't want you to have to shell out more money. I don't need the extra help."

"You do. Now you know that I have always been the type of father who offered more support than mouth, whereas your mother does

support and give you girls mouth." I laughed at
that because it was so true. My daddy was the
laidback one. There was nothing laidback about
my mother. But, in all honesty, to a certain
degree I understood my mother's anger toward
Santana. Had I not dealt with him, some of the
problems I had encountered recently would
have never happened. Like the scene at the
church. Or that crazy girl named Reina messing
up our cars and attacking me. We had never
in all my years of belonging to that church had
any sort of drama like that, or anyone bringing
drama to our doorstep. I knew what happened at
church had humiliated my parents and my sister.
It was exactly why I had to pay those hoodlums
Santana's debt. So they could leave him alone
and stay out of our life.

"Listen. I want you to take care of yourself,
baby. That's all. I'm not going to meddle and tell
you what to do. Just take care of yourself. Got it?"

I smiled and nodded. "I got it, Daddy."

"Now back to business. I'm going to create
a new position. I don't feel like scouting for
someone new so I'm going to hire internally.
They will have to report to you. And once we get
this settled, I don't want to hear anything else
from my employees or you."

"Okay." I knew I had no choice. So I left it alone.

"Use them as an assistant, baby. Let them answer to you. Whatever you can't get to, dump it on them, got it?"

"Yes. And I'm sorry about what happened at church."

My dad looked away when I said the last line, about church. It was like he wanted to comment, but was holding himself back from saying anything. Maybe he didn't want to seem abrasive and intrusive like my mother.

"Santana has made some bad choices, Daddy, but he is really trying to turn his life around. Mom acts like she hates him; just don't look down on us, Daddy."

"I could never look down on you, baby. I love you."

I smiled deeply. I was sure my dimples were showing. It felt good to hear that, especially since my mother and sister were definitely looking down on me. Not to mention my friendship with Arianna seemed like it was over. It felt good to still have my papa on my team.

"Well, I'm going to get going. I won't put this on you since the whole reason we are hiring someone is because you're overwhelmed. So I'll pick the person. Once I make a decision on who I am going to use, I will let you know."

He leaned over and kissed me on my cheek. Then he was out the door.

I was only able to concentrate for another hour before I decided to shut things down and get home to give the cash in my purse to Santana. When I made it home and walked in the door of my house, I saw him pacing back and forth in the living room, his cell phone in his hand.

When he saw me he looked relieved. "Damn, baby. About time you got back here."

"I know. I got the money, so don't worry, Santana." I pulled it out of my purse. "That's twenty thousand right there."

He took a deep breath and gave me a beautiful smile, where all his teeth were exposed. "Thank you, baby." He kissed me on the lips and took the money out of my hands.

"After this, you're done with that, Santana. I'm for real."

"Man, I'm saying . . . I'm done. You just gotta trust me, baby."

"I do. Or else I wouldn't be doing this."

"I know, baby. That's why I love you. You got me. I'm going to have you too . . . Trust."

"Are you going to be okay going to them by yourself? Do you think they will try something?" I truthfully didn't want him anywhere near those guys.

"I'll be fine, babe. Don't worry." He grabbed his keys, stuffed the money in a plastic shopping bag, and was out of the house in a flash.

I was left to sit on the couch and wait for him to come back safely. Or hope he came back safely.

Chapter 16

While waiting for Santana to get back, I cooked dinner. I ended up sautéing shrimp with garlic, onion, and peppers. I also made some rice pilaf and vegetable medley. I had no appetite to eat any of it, not even a few bites.

Once everything was done, I went into my room and lay down. I contributed my loss of appetite to the fact that I feared something bad might happen to Santana. Although he said he would be safe delivering the money to those two guys . . . I didn't know. I just didn't trust them. What if they beat him up? Or, worse, killed Santana? I mean, those men seemed to be really ruthless like Santana had said. They came into a church of all places and physically assaulted him.

But, in all honesty, I knew I couldn't do anything about the situation. He didn't tell me where he was going to meet them and if he did what could I do to help? Nothing. I was a woman with no muscle. I wasn't even good at fighting chicks, let alone a man. And I couldn't call the police because that could get Santana caught up. I had done all I could do, and that was getting him the money. I tried not to worry about it and attempted to go to sleep. My racing mind made that very hard.

Minutes flew to hours. When there was no sign of Santana, I began blowing up his cell with countless texts and calls. I got no response either way. This stressed me out further even though my mother had always taught me not to worry. I couldn't control the dread I was feeling. I cried and bit my nails down to the nubs, really feeling like something had happened to him. Three hours passing were far too many for me. It got to the point that I picked up the phone to call the police and say he was missing. But then I didn't have to because Santana finally walked into the house, calling out, "Babe?"

I jumped up out of the bed and raced to the living room. When I saw him standing there looking around for me, I ran to him and jumped into his arms, saying, "Baby. You're back!"

I hugged him close, heard him laugh, and felt him tighten his arms around me. I was so relieved I got teary-eyed.

"What's wrong, baby?" He slid my body down until I was back standing. He kept his hands wrapped around my waist.

I started sobbing. Those hours I had waited for him to come back I had honestly thought the worst: that my baby wasn't coming back. And now he was here in front of me. Pain moved into joy. He was okay. He was safe and sound.

"I don't know." I wiped the tears that came quickly. "I just kept feeling that you weren't coming back. And now that you're here, I feel so relieved."

"Well I'm for real, for real back. That shit is over now. I'm going to concentrate fully on you. My mind is more at ease now that I don't have that shit on my brain. So I won't be all edgy and moody now, baby." He traced the outside of my lips with one of his index fingers. I kissed the tip of it.

"Now I can work on more legal avenues so I can take care of you, Alexis."

I poked my bottom lip out, thinking, *awww*, at his sweetness. I wished my parents, sister, Arianna, and the members of my church could be flies on my living room wall right now. So they see the beauty of this man. Not just the outer but the inner.

We both sat on the couch. He looked at me and smiled. "Sing me a song, baby."

I closed my eyes and started singing Beyoncé's "1+1." "'If I ain't got something I don't give a damn 'cause I got it with you.'" I continued to sing, hitting all Beyoncé's high notes, like the song was written for me to sing it in that moment to Santana. "'Make love to me, me, me, me. Oh make love to me.'" I had a habit of closing my eyes on high notes. When I opened them I saw that Santana had tears running down his face.

"Baby, don't cry." I grabbed his face between my two hands and pulled him close to me so that I could kiss his tears away.

His expression changed to one of desire. Our mouths opened to each other. Our tongues started battling passionately.

He broke the kiss by saying in a husky voice, "Make love to me, baby."

And I did. We made love with so much fervor. He let me be in control this time. I rode him real slow, giving it to him in a way that made him scream. And as he climaxed he continued to shout, "Alexis, I love you! I love you, Alexis." He kept repeating the same thing, flipping the words around each time.

Then we both went into the bedroom and collapsed on the bed. I slept in his arms peacefully.

As I parked my car across the street from the building my office was located in, I saw Marisol standing near the building, obviously waiting for me. I took my time getting out my car. I wasn't going to rush for her or anyone else. I huffed out an impatient breath as I grabbed my things, and closed and locked my car. I then walked toward the building. She rushed toward me and gushed out with a smile pasted on her face, "Hi, Alexis!"

Despite her enthusiasm, I gave her a mere nod. "Marisol. You need to call before you just pop up here. Your apartment complex is not the only one my father owns you know."

"Oh, no, Alexis. I'm not here for that. Your father came over and talked to me the other day. He hired me as your assistant, to come in and help you out. I tell you, it couldn't have come at a better time and I'm so grateful. With my husband being out of work and in the hospital undergoing his chemo treatments, I sure can use that extra money for my kids."

I frankly did not give a shit about her or her situation. First off, no one told her to have four kids while living in the Montavia Projects (Cerritos was like Beverly Hills to her). Secondly, I wasn't too happy about her tattling to my daddy the day I snapped at her. I had never snapped at her before. I felt I was entitled to one snap. With her being dirt poor and caring for all her kids and dealing with a sick husband, I was sure she blew a head gasket and had snapped on someone once or twice. But she felt the need to tell on *me*. And thirdly, I didn't need someone in my office, all in my face. She seemed nosy.

When I didn't converse with her, she continued. But I pretty much tuned her out. I simply unlocked my office, walked inside, turned on the lights, set my things down, and took a seat behind my desk. She continued to talk. I then started up my computer.

When she finally took a breather I said, "You know, Marisol, I told my father I was fine."

"Well, whatever you need done just let me know. Because I'm here to work."

Marisol stood near the door with her hands clasped together. I guessed waiting for me to welcome her to a seat. I didn't. "There really is nowhere for you in—"

"Oh no. Your father said that he's going to bring a spare desk, chair, and a computer over here for me. Matter of fact, let me call him and see what time they will be bringing it."

Great. I pulled out my cell and sent Santana a text saying I missed him.

She pulled out her phone and I watched her dial my father's number. After a few rings he picked up. "Hi, Mr. Vancamp. It's Marisol. I was calling to see when you were going to bring the items we had discussed."

She waited a few seconds before laughing and said, "Yes! I'm anxious to get started. Yep. I discussed it with my brother, Carlos, and he is going to be in charge of the grounds while I'm here, and he has my cell should he need to ask me anything. Okay, great!" She handed me the phone. "Your dad wants to talk to you."

"Hello?"

"Hey, babe. I got some bad news. I just found out that my aunt passed and your grandmother is not taking it too well. I'm going to fly out there so I won't be back for about two weeks. I told your mother to tell you but she snapped at me and said for me to tell you girls myself. She has been so testy with me lately. So just make sure everything is okay with the buildings and if there are any issues call me."

"Sorry to hear about your aunt, Daddy. And I sure will," I said in a distracted tone. I wanted to get back to texting Santana. I was sorry that my father had lost his aunt, but I didn't really know her so it didn't make me too sad. I just felt a little sad for my daddy.

Forty minutes later, one of my father's workers came to my office, invading my space with all that crap for Marisol's fat ass. She had barely been here an hour and she was already getting on my nerves. Then, I figured, if she was going to be here, why the hell not use her for what she was there for?

I had her running around picking up the rent, putting up FOR RENT signs for vacant units. She was always the one who brought hers to me. While I had always appreciated her taking the extra trip, I felt now it was just her way of brownnosing to my daddy. I also had her check the mail and the abyss of faxes that I hadn't gotten a chance to get to in the past few weeks so I could text back and forth with Santana.

Marisol stood in front of me with a letter in her hand. "Alexis. This is thirty-day notice from Larry Sherman."

"Damn." I put my cell down and grabbed the letter from her. I scanned it quickly. The letter stated that he was putting in his thirty-day notice and vacating his position as manager.

I sighed. With that happening, I knew we were taking a big loss. Larry was over at our complex in Compton. I didn't trust any of the tenants there. And that building was the most challenging of our buildings, because the tenants were often late on their rent. Past tenants were gangbangers and, at one point, someone was literally selling drugs out of the complex. There was a lot of tagging on the property, causing my father to shell out a lot of money for cameras, painters, and even, at one point, security. Police were constantly called over to that building. Although I loved the manager we had at that time, an elderly lady named Diane, we had no choice but to let her go and look for a manager with a stronger presence who could clean house. That was Larry. He was born and raised in Compton. Once we hired Larry, there were never any more issues at that complex. He kept things under control. He was a very strong and efficient manager. The problem was the fact that the fax had been sitting on the machine for the past three weeks and I had not checked it. *Damn.*

"I don't know why he, as manager, didn't call me and tell me he was putting in his notice," I said, trying to take the blame off myself. I didn't need her running and snitching to my dad that I had a big stack of faxes that I hadn't gotten to.

"Well, I checked all your voicemails and he had also called and informed you."

I rolled my eyes at her and snapped, "Well, I'm over six buildings. I am bombarded with work."

"No, I understand. That's why I am here. So what do you want to do?"

"Well, I have a week to figure something out. I'm going to have to start interviewing for the complex, which will be kind of hard because I absolutely do not want anyone who lives in there working for my father's company. None of them can be trusted. I need you to post an ad in the *Penny Saver* and *Press Telegram* about the manager position. Pay is an additional one thousand dollars outside of the rent."

"Okay, I'm on it."

Although I didn't want her in my space or in my face, I had to admit that Marisol was a hard worker. And she did take the load off of me. With her being there, I was guaranteed to be able to get everything done.

"I'm going to head out."

"Well, how will I be able to lock up? Because I planned on staying at least until eight to get this work done," she said. "That way when you come in tomorrow, you will be up to date with everything."

That would be perfect. That way I could sleep in and maybe start taking three days off a week as opposed to two so Santana and I could start traveling more. Maybe it was going to work out, Marisol being there. I pulled the keys for the office off my chain and handed them to her. "Okay."

"What time do you usually come in in the morning, Alexis?"

"Usually by eight."

"Girl." She laughed. "Come in at ten."

"Are you sure?"

She waved a hand. "Yes. I'm an early bird anyhow. I'll get the office started. Don't worry."

"Okay." I shut down my computer, grabbed my things, and left.

"Good night!" she yelled.

"Good night." I said it sincerely and I meant it.

Chapter 17

I went to Fresh & Easy to pick up something to cook for dinner. I had energy and felt refreshed with Marisol doing most of the work. I wanted to make some fish tacos with mango salsa. Santana had never had my fish tacos and I knew it would be the perfect thing to make for him.

I grabbed all the items I needed, paid for them, and went home. I couldn't wait to see my baby.

When I made it home, I discovered the door was unlocked so I slipped in with my things easily. Before I could even get completely in the door I heard, "Hey, sis!"

I damn near dropped what was in my hands when I saw my sister stretched out on one of my couches. "What the fuck are you doing in my house?" I demanded.

She placed her arms behind her head. "Relax. Alexis. And it's *our* daddy's house. Don't you forget that. Working for him doesn't make you the owner of shit you know."

"Stop playing with me!"

"Oh. I'm not, dear sister. Mom is being a real bitch. I decided I didn't want to go back to Spelman, or any other college for that matter, and she is highly upset about that." She sat up on the couch and crossed her legs. I scanned her from head to feet. She was barely dressed in a tank top and a little-ass skirt. Half of her ass was hanging out.

"What does this have to do with you being here?"

"I'm getting to that. Mom kicked me out and said unless I came up with a plan B to dropping out of school I was kicked out." She added, "She said plan B was another school."

"And Dad just let her kick you out?"

"You know Daddy has no freaking backbone. She took my ATM card, too. Thus, here I am. Until I figure out what I am going to do, I shall be here."

"Well, you're not staying," I interjected.

"I've nowhere else to go."

"And you think that is my problem?"

"Baby!" It was Santana.

I softened my voice. "Coming," I called. I set my purse, attaché case, and the bags on the couch. I gave her an evil look before walking into my bedroom.

"*Coming,*" she mocked.

I ignored the bitch and continued walking until I got to my destination. "Hey, baby."

"Hey." He was sitting at my computer desk, on the Internet.

"Don't worry. I'm going to get rid of Bria."

He turned around in the chair. "Naw. Don't do that."

"What do you mean don't do that?" I snapped.

"Calm your voice down." He looked at me with a steady expression.

I took a deep breath and obeyed. "Sorry, babe. But she needs to go. You saw how she acted at dinner and I told you how she carried on in church."

"I know. I don't like the little bitch either. I wish I could slap the shit out of her. You see where I'm at? Away from her ass. But that's your sister. You can't just throw her out with no place to go. Both of y'all are sheltered. She ain't going to survive in the streets. She will end up in a damn trash bag, trying to prove a message to y'all parents. Then you will be kicking yourself in the ass for not letting her stay."

He was right. Despite her mouth and foul attitude, I loved my little sister and I would never forgive myself if something happened to her. Plus, I told myself, the living situation wouldn't be permanent.

"Okay, baby. You're right. I will tell her she can stay."

"Just keep her ass away from me. That way I don't nut up."

Well, since my baby was in school during the day, I knew they wouldn't be around each other all too much. So they wouldn't be going at each other's throats while I wasn't there. Now, when we were all home, I knew it was inevitable that they would get into it. We would just have to deal with it.

When I went back into the living room I saw her stretched out on my couch, on my home phone. "Yeah, girl. I said fuck that. I'm not going back there."

"Bria."

She continued talking like I wasn't standing in front of her calling her name.

"Bria!"

She looked at me and took the phone away from her ear. "What?"

"You can stay. But I'm letting you know now that I'm not putting up with your shit. Neither will Santana. I'm also not going to clean up after your privileged ass."

"Nor will I do any of those things, sister. But don't forget, you're just as privileged as I am. We are cut from the same cloth." She batted her eyelashes at me.

"Yeah, well, I actually graduated from college. And I'm working."

At this point she was back on the phone as if I weren't even talking.

I fumed and grabbed the grocery bags. I went into the kitchen and started preparing dinner. I still didn't want her ass here. I hoped she came to her senses and figured out what she wanted to do with her sad-ass life so she could get the hell out.

I turned my focus off of her and on preparing dinner. I washed the fish, seasoned it, and put it into a frying pan with a little oil so it could cook. Then I started chopping up the mangoes, tomatoes, onion, one small chili pepper, and cilantro for the mango salsa. Once I had everything chopped, I put it into a bowl, squeezed a whole lemon over it, and seasoned it with salt and pepper. I then put it in the fridge so it could chill while the food cooked. I checked the fish; it was cooking on low heat.

"I know, girl!" She was so fucking loud.

I turned on my iPod, which sat on my dock on the kitchen counter, and turned it to Tank. Santana came into the kitchen and slipped behind me. He rubbed on my bottom and kissed me on my neck. I smiled and turned the fish over.

"Ewww. Too much PDA!" she yelled from the living room at us. "You have an infant in here for God's sake!"

I wanted to pull up a video of her on the popular, WorldStarHiphop.com, where she was at a club and slid down a stripper pole with absolutely no panties. Her bush was out for everyone in the club to see and she wasn't the least bit upset about it. She giggled!

Santana felt my body tense up. "Relax, babe. Ignore her ass."

I smiled and kissed him before moving away so I could fry the corn tortillas.

"How long before dinner's done?" he asked.

"Ten minutes."

I poured a little oil in the frying pan and waited for it to heat up before putting two tortillas in the pan. As they began to bubble, I grabbed the *fresco crema* out of the fridge.

"Call me when it's done." He patted my ass and walked out of the kitchen.

"Okay." I flipped the tortillas over, waited another minute, took those two out, and added two more. I repeated this until I had fried a total of eight shells. I knew Santana would want four, I ate two, and I didn't care how many

Bria's ass wanted; she would get two as well, whether she wanted more or not.

Matter of fact, I served her first so she wouldn't eat with us at the table. I had no time for her bullshit. When she walked in the kitchen I silently handed her a plate of food.

"Yummy! Thanks, sis!" When I looked at her she didn't seem like she was trying to be an asshole. She looked like she was sincerely saying it.

So my face softened and I said, "What do you want to drink? Juice or soda?"

"Juice please."

I went to the fridge, grabbed a can of Ocean Spray cranberry juice and handed it to her.

By the time she scarfed her food down, I had Santana's plate ready. I made sure it looked neat and had a nice presentation. I had stuffed plenty of fish in his shells. I set his plate on the table, knowing he had to have his Henny to go with it. I set it out for him also. I had bottled water.

"Babe," I called, "the food is ready."

He came right out. As we ate, my little sister stayed on the phone in the living room, tuning us out. We did the exact same thing. Still, her being there bothered the hell out of me. I knew no matter how nice she was I didn't want her there. I wanted no woman alone with my man. Not even my grandmother. I just didn't.

***

For the next couple days, I observed Marisol. True to her word, she was a really hard worker. Things were back to the order that I used to have before I got so wrapped in Santana and pretty much became a wifey. She took and screened calls for me, checked my email, and, since it was the beginning of the month, she even handled the bank deposits. She went through the same anal ritual I taught her to do, which was photocopying every check and placing it in a file for that specific complex, with the month and year labeled on it. She went over all the maintenance requests and the amounts managers charged to make sure they were accurate and the managers weren't trying to pull the okey doke. She made sure all new tenants were properly screened, running their credit and whatnot. Our policy was that any potential clients had to come see us and apply, to avoid managers putting friends and family members in the vacant apartments and not running a thorough credit check on them.

Marisol was cool with all of this. She was like a clone of the old me. When it came to financial matters, I did still check it all out. I reviewed the photocopies of the checks and made sure every check for each tenant was accounted for, and I then made sure the totals matched the deposits. They did. She did drive-bys to all the properties to make sure the property was clean and the lawns were maintained. It was something I told her she would need to do several times a week. By doing this, it ensured that the managers kept up with their buildings, because they never knew when I was going to pop up. They never wanted to be caught slipping. This kept the buildings clean and tidy, the way my father liked them to be. By her now doing the majority of this, I always came home refreshed with a lot of energy to make love to Santana, and to go on more out-ings during the week when he wasn't in school. Today we were supposed to go for a walk on the beach when I got off.

As I rushed to my door after work, I couldn't help but smell marijuana. Although I didn't touch the stuff, from time to time Santana smoked it. There was also music blasting. I expected to find Santana in the living room, smoking, but not my fast-ass sister sitting right next to him, taking a long pull from a blunt.

Santana had his eyes closed, clearly buzzed without a care in the world, bobbing his head to the music. I slammed the door closed and angrily tossed my purse on the couch.

Santana opened his eyes and saw me. "Hey, babe." They were super tight from his high.

My sister blew out smoke and looked my way. "Hey." She held the blunt out for me to take.

I gave her an evil look before glancing around my living room and taking in how messy it was. It made my blood boil! "Are you serious right now, Bria?"

"Huh?" She looked at me, confused. Her eyes were tighter than Santana's.

"Look at this mess! I'm tired and I warned you already. I'm not your mom and I'm not going to clean up after you."

"Let me go in the room. I don't want to hear this shit and get my high fucked up," Santana said. He got off the couch and brushed past me with no kiss, hug, hi . . . Nothing.

I watched him leave, surprised that he would say that. *He should be on my side.* Was I the only one who saw the mess of my sister's clothes and shoes thrown all around my living room? All of her cosmetics were scattered all over my marble coffee table like she was going out and couldn't figure out what she was going to wear or what shade of lipstick looked the fucking best!

But I didn't want to argue with Santana or for him to feel like I was taking it out on him.

"You're so naïve, big sis. Put your bottom lip back in. He's leaving because when a person has a good high or buzz, the last thing they want is to hear a person bitching, regardless of the reason they are bitching. When he is putting it on you do you want mom bitching in your ear? Huh?"

"Shut the fuck up. You don't ever mention what I do with my man."

"Sorry. I was just using that for an example since he told me you never get high with him, you know."

"Clean up my house now! And you have a room to use so keep your shit out of here!" She had been using Arianna's room since her stay.

She lazily got up off the couch. Once again, she was half dressed. She wore a sports bra and a pair of booty shorts.

"Stop parading yourself in front my man half naked like a whore, understand?"

She got on her knees and shoved all her cosmetics on my table into a Caboodle makeup container. "Girl, please. Insecurity is so not attractive. He ain't looking at me. I'm like his little sister. And you know what? Santana ain't so bad."

I gripped my hands around her throat. "You better get your situation together because you won't be here for that much longer."

"Get your hands off of me." She yanked herself away, but not before I saw the fear in her face. I walked away, pissed the hell off.

The kitchen was also a mess, with various plates and bowls of half-eaten cereal on the table. Bitch was having a *Ferris Bueller's Day Off*. Well, I was the principal today and her ass was going back to class. *If I have to school her ass.*

Despite my anger, I knew I had to make a good meal. Santana would accept no less even if I was tired, and since I didn't want to lose him, I had to always deliver. But it was hard when my sister had managed to agitate the hell out of me. I cooked stuffed pasta shells that were filled with shrimp, spinach, and ricotta cheese. When they were done, I poured marinara sauce over them. I melted real butter along with some crushed garlic in the microwave and poured it over a fresh loaf of French bread.

Santana came into the kitchen and sat down in silence, and I served him. I made myself a light plate and sat down across from him. Bria came in the room with a Love Pink sweat suit on and her hair pulled into a bun. She grabbed a clean plate and piled food on it. She then turned to walk into the living room.

Santana said, "Come eat at the table with us."

My jaw clamped down and my chewing stopped. I tried to keep my agitation off my face as she came looking like some innocent saint to the table.

Why is he being nice to her ass now? I wondered. I guessed she had managed to win him over in the past couple days. I mean the attitude she had shown him back when they first met she didn't show him now. And that was cool because there could have been serious drama between the two of them . . . But still . . . her ass hadn't won me over. As she ate enthusiastically and kept saying that I was such a good cook, I refused to say thank you and just stared down at my plate.

Santana didn't seem to pay me any mind. He ate with relish, tearing it up like my sister. They both ate more than usual. I attributed that to the weed.

"Hey, Alexis?" Bria asked.

"What?"

"Have you heard the new Nicki Minaj song?"

"No." I had.

"You ain't heard it? That shit is banging." She stood and started singing:

> *"Bitches talk shit and they ain't saying nothing.*

A hundred mutherfuckers can't tell me
nothing.
I beez in the trap be beez in the trap."

As she rapped, Santana put down his fork,
tossed his hands in the air, and rocked his head
from side to side.

"Haaaay!" she sang before sitting down.

Santana laughed.

"Hey. Santana, what does that part mean?"

"Trap means a trap house. It's a place where
you sell dope or illegal items. But it's usually
dope."

"Ohhh." She looked so enlightened. "You ever
been in a trap house before?"

He chuckled. "I have."

"Gangsta!" she yelled.

"Girl, you crazy," was all he said between
chuckles.

It was like I wasn't even at the table. But when
Bria caught my evil stare, she stopped talking
and gobbled up the rest of her food. She then left
the table and went to her room.

Not soon after, Santana got up as well, which
disappointed me because I was used to us having intimate dinners, when we both went over
how our days were and what exactly we did. But
I guessed he had no real interest in doing that

with me today. I didn't like it but what could I do? I instead got up and started putting the food away and washed the dishes.

Once I was done, I went into my room. Santana was watching *106 & Park*. He ignored me as I stripped out of my clothes and put on my robe to take a shower.

"How was school?" I asked him. Truthfully, it wasn't what I wanted discuss. I wanted to vent to him about my sister. But I remembered what my sister said about me fucking up his high. I didn't want to do that or seem petty to him. I mean, they were only minor things that had happened. She had made a mess in my living room that she cleaned up without giving me lip and she had smoked weed with my man. They both were grown. I knew it wasn't Santana's first time smoking in the house; I was pretty sure it wasn't hers either. They weren't huge deals for me to still be tripping off of. Maybe I was jealous to see them two having fun together without me.

"I didn't go in today."

I tied the sash on my robe. "Why not?"

"I didn't feel like it. That's why not."

"Oh, well, I thought maybe you weren't feeling well or something."

He ignored me and continued to watch Beyoncé gyrate on the screen.

I walked into the bathroom to shower. I turned on the showerhead, let it get hot, and stepped inside. I lathered myself up with my Victoria's Secret strawberries and champagne body wash. As I did this, I wondered why he was being so short with me. I knew I had a bit of a 'tude because of my sister, but I was trying to let it go and he was still being like, *whatever*. We had been getting along so well, I really didn't want any problems or tension between us. Maybe he didn't approve of the way I was treating my sister. If that was the case, I would let up on her. Although I had definitely been more focused on what I wanted to accomplish than she had, I had to admit I made some mistakes in my earlier years. So I couldn't act like I didn't identify with my sister completely.

My parents always said my little sister was more of a free spirit and I was always more grounded. At the age of four, she had run away from home because my mother didn't make her chicken fingers and fries for dinner. At seven, during a ballet recital, she switched her performance song from the music of *Swan Lake* to "Shake That Monkey," by Too Short. It had mortified the hell out of my poor parents. She crashed my mother's car when she was only fourteen. My sister had some seriously PK rebellion issues.

And truthfully, I didn't want her in my home. It didn't mean I didn't love her. I just didn't want her around. She was a damn ticking time bomb.

I rinsed off, got out of the shower, and lotioned my body down with shea butter cream. I then put on my silk nightgown that was hanging on the door. I really wanted Santana to make love to me.

But when I came out of the bathroom and into our room I saw he wasn't in bed.

When I went to go look for him, I was surprised to find him standing in the doorway of my sister's room. I stood behind him and saw my sister had stripped down to her underwear, which was a thin-ass thong, and her big ass was in the air. She wore nothing else.

I tried to remain calm. "Baby, what are you doing?"

He turned around and looked at me. "What do you think I'm doing? Lusting on your sister huh?"

I swallowed hard. "Yes. That's what it looks like."

"You would think some simple shit like that. We smoked some Kush. That's a heavy weed. I just want to make sure she not passed out. I didn't think you thought so low of me."

He walked off and ignored me when I called his name.

Chapter 18

I couldn't sleep the previous night, which caused me to oversleep, so I didn't make it to the office until twelve. Santana wouldn't touch me and I lay in bed for hours before sleep actually took over.

When I woke up I saw Santana had left for school. My lateness caused me to miss three of the interviews Marisol had scheduled for the management position of the Compton complex. This agitated the shit out of me because I felt Marisol should have just gone on ahead and interviewed the candidates herself, instead of feeling the need to tell me she had sent three different people home.

"Oh, well. I have people lined up all day to interview. That's their loss."

Every hour on the clock, I was looking at a different face and asking them the same damn questions. My mind stayed on Santana and our problems from the day before, which made it difficult for me to focus on what any of them were saying as they sat across from me. By three o'clock, I was drained and itching to leave the office.

I told Marisol to take charge and if she needed me, she could hit my cell.

"But you have some more interviews lined up."

I packed up my things. "You interview them. And whoever you think is the best candidate, let me know."

"I have no real experience with that. I'd hate to pick the wrong person."

"You'll be fine, Marisol," I said curtly. "Remember you are my backup. My right-hand man. I have to go." I walked out of my office quickly.

Trying to find a way to fix the problems we had from the night before, I went shopping for my baby. I bought him a pair of new tennis shoes, and two pairs of True Religion jeans. I also bought him a Michael Kors watch.

Day turned into evening and before I went home and surprised Santana with his goodies, I went to pay my mother a visit. I hadn't been back to my mother's house in a while. I knew she was still upset with me because I was still with Santana, after what had happened at church.

Mom would have to get over it. Santana wasn't this bad guy she thought him to be. I felt my mom should be a little ashamed of herself for judging him. Only God was supposed to judge. Like I said before, every saint has a past and every sinner has a future.

She answered the door with a frown, but let me inside.

"Hi, Mom." I pecked her on her right cheek before sitting on the couch. She gave me a curt nod and walked over to the couch across from me. She had the news on and was sipping on some tea. My dad was still out of town. "So how are things?"

She looked at me and gave a bitter laugh. "How are things? Let's see. My oldest daughter—who is breathtakingly beautiful, graduated cum laude, has the voice of an angel with the world literally at her feet—is obsessed with a man who belongs in the *gutter*. And no matter what I say or what he does, she just won't leave the bastard alone." She paused. "My baby has dropped out of school and refuses to do anything with her life. She is so passionate about amounting to nothing that she will be homeless to prove it. Then there's my husband. Despite the fact that he says he is not having an affair, I am getting sick, pathetic phone calls from someone who likes to throw in my face the fact that she is screwing my husband. It's to the point that I have to turn off my phone. The last time they called, they had a porno playing in the background. A woman was yelling, 'Fuck me! Fuck me! Fuck me!' Of all the times for this to be going on, you know we have our annual anniversary party coming up. I should invite the bitch calling me, if I knew who she was."

I laughed at my mother's dark humor. "Mom. Don't think that dad's cheating. He's not."

"If he is, that is at the bottom of my list. My babies are what is stressing me out the most. I can't believe out of all I just said that is the only part you responded to."

"Because no matter what I say about Santana, you are convinced he is a bad guy. But, Mommy, he is in school, he takes good care of me, Mom. You don't have to worry. He even said he wants to have it to where I don't have to work for Daddy anymore."

She didn't look convinced at anything I had just said. So I left that part alone.

"And as for Bria, that is what I came to talk to you about. She is staying with me."

"What?" My mother looked surprised.

"You heard me right. I don't want her there, Mom. I want my own privacy. She is lazy and doesn't want to do anything."

"I don't want you living with that man and now my baby is there too?"

She was going to go in on Santana again and I didn't want to hear it. "Mom! That is so past the point you—"

Someone started banging on the front door.

"What in the hell?" My mother stood up and walked to the door to answer it.

"It's probably a solicitor." I closed my eyes, irritated to the fullest.

I heard my mother unlock and open the door. "Yes?"

All I heard was, "Where she?"

I froze. I recognized that accent.

I turned around, alarmed. But it was too late; they barged into my mother's house. It was the two Jamaican dudes. They had brought five other dudes with them.

"Who are you and what are you all doing barging in my goddamn house?" my mother demanded.

"Dun know?" Dylan was all in my mother's face, causing her to back up. "Dun know?"

I stood and looked at them fearfully.

That's when my mother finally realized who he was. "You're the one who barged into our church! Talking about some *dun know*. Yes, I don't know why you guys are here, so you need to leave before I call the police!"

He pulled out a gun from his back pocket and pointed it at my mother. But he looked over at me. "Me must speak to she, 'cause she da Bupps."

"Bupps?" my mother asked. She looked from him to me.

I was confused as well as to what he was talking about, but I was afraid to speak as they encircled my mother and me.

"In me country, bupps be sugar daddy. But he not that. She be that." He pointed at me. "Santana be sweet boy."

His terminology had me really confused.

"What does that have to do with you barging in my goddamned house?"

"Me real live bwo ya know?"

"What?

He pulled back the safety on his gun, making my mother and me scream.

"Me real gangsta!" he yelled at the top of his lungs.

One of the men pulled the phone cord out of the wall while another snatched my purse and went through it.

Before we could do anything, they started destroying my mother's house. They busted my parents' sixty-inch flat-screen TV, the expensive paintings on the walls. They broke the real crystal by knocking down the clear glass case it all resided in. It came crashing down, causing the glass case to break and the pieces to fall to the floor. The pieces that were still intact were stomped on, making my mother cry. One of them even took a knife out of his pocket and stabbed my mother's costly couches.

My mother and I crawled away and hid in a corner of the room.

As they continued destroying the living room, Dylan said, "Bumbaclot pussy clot Santana. Me know you got good shit here."

My mother screamed and I looked on, still scared to speak. I couldn't understand why they were doing this. Santana had paid them.

The house was a complete mess and everything in it was destroyed, down to my mother's coffee table. They had jumped on until it collapsed into several broken pieces. Then they pulled out their dicks and peed all over the walls and on the white carpet. "You bas—"

I put my hand over my mother's mouth so she didn't say anything that would anger them.

Dylan spat on the floor and said. "Tell Batty boy me want all me money tomorrow. Not vex me again!" They walked out the door.

"What is this?" my mother yelled at the top of her lungs. "I know that bastard is behind this! I know it, he said his name."

While my mother yelled I searched in the clutter for my purse. Once I found it, I ran out of the house, despite my mother yelling for me to come back. I didn't know what Santana had done, but I assumed he didn't give them all of their money and I was pissed! By him doing this he endangered both my parents. I raced home, enraged. I was going to get to the bottom of this.

Chapter 19

When I walked into my house, I saw my sister poke her head out of the kitchen.

"Hey, big sis! I'm making burgers and packing on the *cheddar cheese*."

I ignored her and went into my bedroom. Santana sat at the computer.

In that moment, I didn't care about making him mad. I raised my voice and snapped, "What did you do? Why didn't you give them all the money?"

He turned around and looked at me like, *damn, I'm caught.*

"Do you have any idea what they just did to my parents' house?"

"Sit down, baby." He had his head in both his palms.

"No!" I had tears in my eyes. "You have no idea what I had to do to get all that money. I did it to help you and you shitted on me, Santana. I can't blame my mother for hating you now and when my dad finds out, he will too! Why would you do that? What did you do with the money and how much did you short them?"

"No, baby. It's not what you think. Yes, I shorted them by half of it. I gave half real money, the other half counterfeit bills."

I gasped. "Why?"

"Because! Look, I was stressed out by the fact that as a man I wasn't bringing any money into this household. And remember when I said I was working on holding you down?"

I nodded, remembering it, but separating the sweet feelings it had brought that day in that moment because I was furious with Santana.

"Okay, well, I got an email from a man in Africa."

"Why do I *already* not like how this sounds?"

"Just listen, baby. He said the government out there was crooked and was trying to persecute him by taking his inheritance. He needed someone to put the money from his inheritance into their bank account and he would give me one hundred thousand dollars if I did it. All I needed was to send him ten thousand dollars for the fund's conversion."

"Santana! That's a scam. Everyone gets those emails. Why didn't you ask me? I would have easily told you that before you threw away ten thousand dollars."

"Why would a nigga from another country do some shit like that?" he asked naïvely.

"To scam people out of their money, and that is what he did to you."

"Shit," he mumbled. "And all this time I been waiting to get the email saying they have sent the funds over. Damn!"

I didn't say anything. I was set back even more now. I still owed my dad and I hadn't put it back yet. Now I would have to come up with another $10,000? If I didn't they weren't going to leave the situation alone.

I looked away.

"I'm so sorry, babe. I fucked up. But I was only trying to make our situation better." He slapped his hands together angrily. "Man!"

"Just stop. I will figure this out in the morning. Let me sleep please."

I pulled off my shoes and clothes and lay down in the bed. Santana got behind me and we spooned. I didn't say much to him as he rubbed my back because I was pissed at him for what he did. I knew he was doing it because he wanted to make our situation better. But the reality of the situation was that what he did was dumb and put us in a rut. The last thing I wanted to do was take money from my father again.

A few minutes later, I heard my sister yell that the burgers were done.

When Santana asked me if I wanted him to bring me one, I told him no. He got up out of the bed and went into the kitchen.

I got up, went into the bathroom, popped an Ambien, and went back to lie down. With all my racing thoughts about this mess I knew I wouldn't be able to sleep without one.

The next morning, I got up and threw on what I wore the day before because it was on the floor near the bed and just easier to grab.

I went into the office and swept right past Marisol, ignoring her when she said, "Good morning!"

Without even bothering to sit down, I unlocked the safety box on my desk that had petty cash, blank checks, and an ATM card. Since I was my father's accountant, my name was on the card. I threw in into my purse, planning to get the money off of the card. I didn't have time to pull from separate accounts to cover up the big withdrawal; I would do it later.

As I prepared to walk out of the office and go to the bank, Marisol yelled, "Wait, Alexis."

I huffed out an impatient breath, turned, and looked at her.

"As you know, Larry's last day was yesterday. I have narrowed it down to two different people for the complex in Compton. I am still waiting for a background check on both of them."

"You mean to tell me that we have no one presiding over that fucking property yet?" I demanded.

Her eyes were wide at my cursing at her. "Well, I did all the interviews yesterday. I wanted you to make the final decision on who you want."

"We need that manager's spot filled. Just pick someone. You should be able to differentiate between a decent and bad person without the damn background check that we have no time to wait for. It's a matter of common sense. You're old enough to make a sound decision aren't you? You are far from a baby." I yanked the office door open. "Far! Make a decision, fill the spot, or that's your job," I threatened. I was sick of her weak, indecisive old ass. I had other shit to worry about.

I went to the bank got the money. I then texted Santana and told him to meet me at the house. To ensure that he dropped all of it off this time I planned on going with him.

Although he didn't want me to, I insisted.

I rode alongside Santana as he traveled to the jungles, scared for my life. I didn't even want to get out of my car. But to be assured this was done and over with, I followed him into the home of Dylan.

When we entered, there were so many people smoking weed it was making my head hurt. They were blasting music and partying like it was a Friday night. One of the guys even tried to push up on me as if he forgot he was one of the ones who ruined my mother's beautiful living room. I brushed him off and stood by the door as Santana passed the money off to Dylan. Once it was counted and determined to be the total ten grand, we were allowed to leave.

I was relieved as we drove back home that the shit was over. Dylan now had what he wanted so he had no other reason to bother us ever again.

Santana broke up silence in the car by asking, "You still mad at me, baby? You still love me?"

"No and yes. Always," I said in a quiet tone. I was still angry though.

He smiled as he steered and used his free hand to grab my hand and kiss it. "Damn. I love you for holding me down, baby. As soon as I finish school and I get a job, I got you, baby."

I smiled, my anger slowly melting the more he talked.

"I promise not to do anything else stupid. And you got my word. I'm going to stay the fuck off the Internet!"

I tossed my head back and laughed, despite the situation.

Santana joined me in the laughter, saying, "Man! What I wouldn't do to find that lying-ass African nigga and kick his ass."

"Good luck on that."

"I'm saying."

I didn't bother going back to work that day. Santana had a craving for some greasy, messy burgers and fries. So we ate at Master Burgers on Western. Then we went home, bypassed my sister, and went into our room.

I stripped down, ignoring my mother blowing up my cell phone and the text from her saying she wanted Santana out of my father's house. If my daddy wanted him out he would come put him out, but my daddy hadn't even contacted me about the incident. If he wasn't going to bring it up to me then I wasn't going to bring it up to him. In fact, I turned off my phone and made passionate love to Santana again and said I would worry about any other pressing matters another time. I simply drowned in my man.

Chapter 20

I let a week pass before taking my mother's call. I was in my car, on the way to work. The two times she had stopped by to see me, luckily I was gone. One of those times, Santana was home. My sister Bria had called me and said it was pretty bad. My mother cursed him out for a good fifteen minutes. Bria said Santana just sat there and stared out into space. I was relieved that he didn't argue back with my mother. And when my sister refused to leave with my mother, Bria said my mom called her an "ungrateful bitch." My mother had even called the police to get Santana out. But they informed her that, according to the new law, in order for her to get Santana out, she would need to go to the courthouse and evict him, and that could take months.

I had dodged her for a week because I didn't want to deal with my mother being so pissed off. I also figured after a week my mother would have not only calmed down but she would also get her house back together and replace all that was destroyed. I also knew once she did this, I wouldn't have to give her any money for the damage.

When Santana spoke to me about her visit, he told me that we should move out of my father's house. He said he had the hookup on a low-income apartment in the Carmelitos Housing Complex, if we came up with $500. I looked at him like he was insane and said no. There no way I was going to live in the projects.

I answered my mother's call as I drove to work. "Mommy. I'm so sorry for what happened last week. I'm going to replace all that was lost."

"Save it! You're selfish just like your sister. Don't worry. I made a police report about it! But I don't want to even think about that day. I have relived it over and over again, and each time, I'm no less furious." She paused. "Has your father even bothered to call you?" she asked me.

"No, he hasn't." And that was the truth. My dad had been out of town since the incident happened. I was sure my mother had called him and informed him of what went down but he hadn't called me, thank God.

"I told him that I want Santana out of that house! I don't care where he goes. He needs to get out."

"Mom! No! Listen. I'm sorry for what happened but I can't put him out."

"He needs to leave and if you don't have him out by—"

My line clicked. I looked at the caller ID. It was Marisol.

"Mom, let me call you back." I clicked over and demanded, "What is it?"

"We have a problem. You need to meet me at the complex in Compton! I'm there now."

"Shit." I busted a U-turn and hopped on the 91 Freeway. I exited at Santa Fe Boulevard, made a right, and drove, toward my father's complex.

I saw Marisol standing near her busted-up Honda Civic. I cut my eyes from her as she pointed at the complex. I scanned the building and gasped. Someone had tagged on every outside wall of the complex.

"Shit!" I got out of my car, slammed the door, and stormed up to Marisol. "When did this happen?" I demanded.

"Last night. There is more to the story. More to see. You should come have a look for yourself."

I followed her. Distressed was the only word to describe how I felt when I saw the inside of the building. The tagging was inside as well. There were several windows that were busted. The railing on the stairs was bent back and there was trash thrown all on the ground. Someone had busted the sprinkler system and water was splattering everywhere.

I put my hands to my face and looked around. "Where is the manager you hired?"

"He's here."

I walked with Marisol upstairs to the manager's apartment. I didn't even bother knocking. I open the door and stormed inside.

The worthless excuse of a man was a tall, black square-looking dude with glasses. He had the look of a coward. He was going back and forth in his living room, placing items in a big cardboard box. Was he leaving?

"Why are you in your apartment and not fixing the problems a manager is supposed to fix?" I snapped, shaking my head in disgust. "My father's building looks like crap!"

"Well, it's on you now. I'm leaving. I will be out of here in the next two hours."

"And this is who you hired!" I demanded of Marisol.

She shrugged. "He seemed like he had integrity."

"Integrity! He is worthless. We needed someone with street smarts! You knew that."

"No. I didn't," she said defensively. He continued piling his stuff in boxes. "That's why I wanted you to do this."

"You really have no common sense, Marisol. It's Compton!"

She started crying. "I'm really sorry, Alexis. What can I do to do to fix this? I feel really bad."

"Let me think." I took a deep breath and tried to figure this out. Marisol and I could paint over the graffiti and clean up the building. I would just have to call the handyman we used to put in new glass windows and call the gardener to fix the sprinkler system.

I turned to the manager. "We will be back in an hour. I want you and your shit gone and you off these premises! Don't expect a good reference from me. Let's go, Marisol."

She followed me out of the apartment.

Marisol and I went to Lowes. We stocked up on paint, rollers, and paint brushes. I even bought a coverall suit for myself, threw on my tennis shoes I kept in my trunk, and we went to work painting the outside of the building. It was smarter for us to do it ourselves. In the past, I had hired painters. But since I had taken money out of the account to pay back the Jamaicans, the money from that account remained unaccounted for, so I needed to preserve as much as possible. By not hiring painters, I had done this. I called Santana to see when he got out of school but he didn't answer. Marisol's husband, who had just gotten out of the hospital a few weeks ago, came instead and helped us by getting on a ladder and getting the spots we couldn't reach. We got up all the trash and her older brother, who looked like a hoodlum, was nevertheless very helpful to us by repairing the sprinkler system. I was able to save money by him fixing it. He even repaired the railing for me, which he fixed with a crowbar. The only real big expense was replacing the broken windows.

By the time we finished, it was late. I figured that I could have Santana come and take over until I filled the spot. I was sure his presence would help keep the hoodlums away. I texted him and told him I would be home pretty late after midnight. I wanted to stick around and monitor the place. But I was so tired I wanted to go home and get into bed. Marisol saw it.

"Go home, Alexis. Don't worry. My brother and I will stay tonight. And my younger brother is on the way for extra backup. Don't worry, he is major muscle. And if we see anything suspicious we will call the police. I'll make it back to the office in time to open up first thing in the morning. Don't worry. I will also rerun the ad. You need to go get your rest. You look like you are about to fall out."

Truthfully, I was beat. I had paint all over my face and in my hair. I just wanted to soak in the tub. "Okay. If you are sure you got this. Remember, if you see anyone suspicious, call the police."

"I will, don't worry."

"Thank you, Marisol. I don't know what I would do without you." I meant that. I realized I could not completely blame her for the fiasco. I was the one who told her to pick and she chose to the best of her ability. He was weak sauce, and clearly, he had absolutely no presence, or else the hoodlums would have thought twice before doing what they did. And with all the hard work she had been doing, she was entitled to make a mistake.

Chapter 21

I was so beat that I had no energy at all to cook. I didn't feel like being creative or driving far out to get something for dinner. I ended up getting a pizza and a six-pack of Coke, and drove home. It was a far cry from the Harold & Belle's I had planned on picking up but Santana would just have to understand. I had a very rough day. I always made sure we ate well so I needed a break today.

I unlocked the door and held the pizza box up to my chin as I turned the doorknob, trying not to drop the cans of soda and my purse that were in my other hand. Just in case Santana was asleep, I tried not to be loud as I stepped into the house and kicked the living room door closed.

I turned and the sight I saw before me horrified me to no end.

My sister. Bria. She was naked and she was on top of Santana, riding him.

I watched her toss her head back and moan deep in her throat.

Everything I was holding came crashing down to the floor as I let out a loud, piercing scream.

Bria looked up and so did Santana. But before she could get off Santana's lap, I rushed forward and grabbed her by her hair. "You fucking whore!"

"Baby!" Santana said.

But it was too late. I yanked her off of him and dragged her until she was on my carpet. In her nakedness, I punched and punched and punched her until her face was all bloody. I wanted to kill that bitch. She tried to get away from me, begging, "Alexis, stop please!"

But I wouldn't let her get away. I wasn't a good fighter but I sure was whipping her ass. I straddled her and started slamming her head into the ground. She tried to scratch my face but I tilted my head back so she couldn't. I then grabbed her hands in one of mine and went back to punching her. When I started strangling Bria, Santana grabbed my arms and pulled me off of her.

"I'm going to kill you, you fucking whore!" I tried to get away from Santana but he held me in a tight grip.

She scrambled away and pulled on a dress that was on the floor near the couch. I yanked myself out of Santana's arms. I ran into her room and started grabbing all her things: her purse, shoes, clothes, and jewelry.

I heard her on the phone saying, "Mom, I'm coming home."

I rushed back out of her room with a handful of her stuff. "Yeah, go home, bitch!" I yelled. I walked outside and threw all her items on the sidewalk. When I went back inside, she was sniffling on the couch like she was hurt or something.

I marched back toward her bedroom again, sobbing all the way. I couldn't get the image of them out of my head. Santana tried to block me.

"Get out of my way!" I raged.

"I'm saying, baby, calm down."

I shoved him out of my way. I grabbed more things and took another trip outside with more of her items. I came back again and got the last of her things. By this time she was outside, picking up her stuff and putting it in her car. I threw the rest of it on the curb.

Then I ran back inside and got my broom. I ran back outside and started hitting her in the head with the broom. "Get out of here!" I yelled at the top of my lungs.

She covered her head with her hands and screamed.

But I kept beating her in her head until she opened the door to her ghetto-ass Charger and dived inside. I kept hitting the car with the broom until she backed out of my driveway and sped down the street.

Once the tramp was gone, I then stalked back into the house. I looked for Santana and saw he wasn't in the living room. I walked into the bedroom and saw him standing near the bed as if he was now waiting for me to retaliate against him.

I walked up to him and slapped the shit out of him. "How could you sleep with my sister huh? You lying, cheating bastard! How the fuck could you?" I continued to beat him in his face. "I try my best by you to make you happy. I make love to you just the way you want me to. I cook the best foods I can. I make sure you have everything you need and you do me like this. Get out!" I punched him in his chest. He backed up a little.

"Get out!" I punched him again.

But this time he took steps forward, causing me to back up into the wall, but he wouldn't hit me. "Baby. Sorry."

I slapped him over and over again, yanking at his hair to inflict whatever pain I could on him. "Get out." I punched him in the chest again.

He hemmed me against the wall and continued to let me hit him.

"I hate you!" He kissed me. I drew back and punched him in his face again. "Get out!"

He kissed me again and I hit him again. But he continued to give me kisses all over my face, whispering, "I'm sorry, baby."

I felt myself weaken at his lips. "Get . . ."

He moved in and started kissing me on my lips, repeating, "Sorry."

I retuned the kiss, then tried to push him away, but he was relentless and each kiss brought my rage down a notch until I was kissing him back with the same fervor. "Why can't I hate you!"

I twisted his shirt in my hands. Then I went to cup his face for a kiss, then went back to twisting his shirt in my hands. I was fighting, then giving in to him. "Why can't I hate you! *Why?*"

"Because you love me, baby."

"I don't want to," I sobbed. "You hurt me. You've done me so bad, Santana."

"Let me fix it, baby."

"No." I slapped at his hands as he stripped me of my clothes. He started rubbing all over me, making my body betray me. He had slept with my sister and here I was against this wall, moaning because of his touch, his lips. And not just because of this but because of how I felt in my heart. I loved him even after he had done the ultimate betrayal. And what he was doing to me, I honestly didn't want him to stop. This shit was fucking up my thoughts, actions, and my sound decisions. He was making me an idiot. A dumb, naïve bitch. A pitiful bitch. One who other women would look at and say, "Damn. She is just plain stupid." Why I couldn't just break away? Because I loved him.

He lifted me in the air and ate my pussy. When he flipped me around and fucked me from behind on that wall, my eyes rolled back in my head and I threw my pussy right back at him. I knew as I came (and I came hard) that there was no way I was ever getting rid of this man. I was hooked. No one could do anything about it. Although this actuality was very scary, for the moment, I accepted this . . . I didn't really see anything that I could do about it. Like I said, he had me hook, line, and sinker. And I was sinking.

Although I told myself that it was best that I didn't even bring it up, Santana sleeping with my sister, I knew I had to have at least one conversation with him as to what happened.

"She kept walking around half naked and shit. I was high as fuck that day from some bomb-ass

Stress and here comes her ass with an X pill. I took it and the shit had me so fucked up I was out of it. The whole time she was on top of me it was like her head was spinning like some exorcism shit. That was some potent-ass ex. But that shit . . . What happened between me and her don't mean nothing. She don't mean shit to me because you have my heart, baby. And I was fucked up! I didn't mean to hurt you, that's for sure."

What a conniving bitch. What I believed was that she did what she did on purpose to hurt me. I was glad I put my foot down and kicked her out of my damn house. But I was still hurt. The hurt came from both directions. Santana's part and my sister's. I found my sister to be the main culprit though. I mean, Santana was a man, and you are throwing vajayjay at him; what do you expect? He's not going to try it? That bitch gave him drugs and deliberately seduced him. Just trash! That's what she was. I wasn't justifying Santana's part, just stating the facts. Our relationship was repairable but not my relationship with my sister. Bitch was dead to me. She just couldn't stand to see me happy! She had to taste the ripe fruit. I knew it was tempting to be around him. I mean he was drop-dead gorgeous and sexy as hell. But that was a line she should have never crossed.

"Well, I'm definitely hurt by what you did, Santana. But at the same time, I get it; the bitch set you up to deliberately hurt me."

"I'm saying, you know I wouldn't have touched your sister if I wasn't lit. I'm damn near thirty years old."

"I don't want to hear any more about it. I need to get it out of my mind so I can move forward. I love you and I think this is repairable."

"I love you too, baby. Only you. I mean you, my boo. No other bitch will change that. "

It was a relief to hear that it was just sex, because to tell the truth, when I saw them starting to bond, it made me jealous. I just never anticipated them having sex.

Just then I got a text from my father saying he was coming back home tomorrow, and asking how was everything going. I wondered if I should tell him what happened at the Compton complex. Then I thought better. I sent a text saying everything was good. I then called Marisol.

She answered cheerfully. "Hey, Alexis."

"Hi. How is the building?"

"Everything is fine. You know I wanted to talk to you about my older brother. I would have recommended him for the job initially, but he has a record and I know you're strict on that."

"Okay. Well you know what, I trust your judgment. If he is capable of managing the complex, hire him. We can make an exception this time. Just this time," I said firmly.

"Really!" she gushed out.

"Yes," I said in a distracted tone.

"Thank you, Alexis. I will let him know. He is a really good worker."

I looked at Santana and tried to figure out something fun we could go do today. *Maybe a nice drive to San Diego would be cool.* To get our minds off what had happened the night before.

"Will you be okay on your own today? I need to take the day off."

"Oh, sure!"

"Great. I'll see you tomorrow."

I ended the call.

Santana yanked me so I fell back in his arms. I laughed. "You feel like driving today?"

"If that will put a smile on your face, yeah."

"Let's go to Sea World."

"I ain't never been. I always wanted to go though."

Aww. My baby missed out of so much growing up. "Well, get up. We will go today."

He looked at me and said, "And you question how much I love you. How can a nigga not? Man, you are that *bitch*. Never doubt that shit."

I smiled deeply at him.

We took a quick shower together, got dressed, I packed a few snacks, and we set out for Sea World.

Chapter 22

The next day, I was refreshed and cheerful. I had managed to put the incident with my sister and Santana behind me. Anytime the image of them screwing flashed before my eyes, I remembered his words: how he said that he loved me and no other bitch mattered. *I am that bitch.*

When I got to my office, I noticed that Marisol was acting very strange. I thought it was weird because I was at a point where I had no more issues with her and I was happy she was working for me. Yet, I couldn't ignore how bizarre she was acting.

She didn't bother saying good morning to me, first off, and she had this odd look on her face when we made eye contact, while she talked on the phone.

As I sat down at my desk, I heard her whisper into the phone, "She's here."

I set my stuff down. "Morning."

She ended the call quickly, placed her hands together, and took a deep breath. "Alexis, we need to talk."

I arched an eyebrow at her. "Okay. Talk."

"As you know, I have been assisting you for the past month and a half, and I have been really doing a lot of your work. Which I don't mind. I wanted to make things easier on you and your father. So one thing I did was start ledgers for every complex. I started each one from year to date. I wanted to make sure every account was properly balanced and all funds and expenses were accounted for. The problem was, I noted there was a huge withdrawal taken out of the Cerritos complex. Then what was odd was there were staggered amounts taken out of the other accounts and the huge sum taken out of Cerritos complex was put back. This was fine because it was put back. But the staggered amounts of withdrawals taken out of all the accounts had no receipts or invoices to explain what the withdrawals were for. What was funny was that when I added the amounts together just to have a total of missing assets, it equaled the amount that was taken out the Cerritos complex." She pulled off her glasses. "Then there was another withdrawal for ten thousand."

I was startled by all she knew. But I kept my cool. "What are you trying to say?"

"I think I've said it. You've been stealing from your father."

I stood from my seat. "You ungrateful bitch! Who the fuck do you think you are, implying that I would steal from my father?" I raged.

She placed a hand to her chest. "Calm down."

"I'm going to personally call my father and have him escort your fat, nosy, slandering ass off the premises."

Her eyes got watery and her lips trembled at my insults. "Well, he is already on the way. I called him. I am no longer comfortable working for him knowing what I know about you."

"First off, I didn't steal anything from my father! Secondly, the one who will be in hot water is you." I aimed a finger at her. "You have obviously been snooping and found some kind of way to access the accounts. Probably so you can steal to feed your bastard children."

She gasped. "How dare you call my kids bastards! And if you want to know, your father gave me access to all the accounts. He trusted the both of us. Maybe that was the mistake. *You* can't be trusted."

"Get the fuck out of my office!"

She stood to her feet. "I will wait outside until your father gets here so he can see for himself what you have been doing!" She walked out.

I panicked and loaded up my computer. I had to figure out something so my dad didn't discover that I had taken $20,000 from his accounts. Maybe I could show that the money was pulled to that bitch's building and convince my dad that she had taken it. But I was shocked to discover that when I tried to log on, it said, Access denied!

Now I was filled with fury. I wanted to kick her fat ass.

Yes. I knew that I had taken money from my father, but it wasn't her place to spy on me. I had every intention of giving my father his money back! With her meddling, I was going to have to come up with a lie to tell him!

My father walked into my office with that bitch in tow.

"Daddy, she is lying and spying on me. Give me a chance to explain. I think she took the money and is trying to frame me!"

He held his hands up at me and said sternly, "Be quiet." She went behind her desk and he followed her over.

"But—"

"Marisol has worked for me for over ten years. And she is a good employee."

As she went over all the ledgers and each account they accompanied, I sat there looking stupid. My father looked so disappointed in me. I looked away.

"What do you have to say for yourself?"

I put my head down. "I needed the money and I had every intention of putting it back. I'm sorry."

"Baby, you are my first born and I love you. But you stole twenty thousand dollars from me and you were willing to put it on Marisol, an innocent person. What if I were to believe you and fire her? Her family would be out on the streets. Did you know her husband is back in the hospital? I don't know what you were thinking, baby. If you needed extra money, depending on what it was for you could have come to me."

Key words: depending on what it was for. If I had told him it was for Santana's debt he wouldn't have given it to me. That's why I took it.

"I don't know what is going on in your head, but, baby, I'm going to have to let you go."

I gasped. "What? Daddy, no." Tears started slipping from my eyes even though they were closed.

"I'm sorry, baby. Marisol is going to cut you a check, but it will be for four weeks' pay to hold you over until you find another job."

I was bawling as my father spoke.

"I don't know if you did this fo . . ." He stopped speaking and cleared his throat. I knew he was finally going to go in on me about Santana.

But he didn't. He said instead, "I hope no one is negatively influencing you. But I know you're grown and you are going to make your own decisions no matter what I say. I just hope you remember all the things your mother and I have taught you."

"Give me another chance," I begged.

"I can't. The fact of the matter is that when it comes to finances, I will never trust you again. You are still my baby." He started crying between words. "I love you. But you have to go. I have too much going on. There are things eating at me . . . I don't need this."

I covered my face with my hands, feeling horrible for letting my daddy down so bad that he didn't even want to look at me. I bowed my head and cried into my forearms.

He continued to speak. "In two weeks, your mother is throwing our anniversary party. She said you don't return her calls so she wanted me to let you know that if you bother to show up, not to bring Santana."

I was no longer listening to my father. My focus was on Marisol. "I hope your husband dies!"

"Alexis!" my father shouted at me.

I grabbed my purse, not bothering with my attaché case, and ran out of his office. I threw myself into my car and sobbed for a good fifteen minutes before I drove away.

Chapter 23

I had to go on a series of seven interviews before I was able to get a job. And it wasn't where I hoped to get one. Instead of a job at Chase Bank or a position as a CPA, I was hired at Nick's Checks Cashing on Atlantic Boulevard, in North Long Beach. I brought home peanuts: a measly $650 every two weeks. When I worked for my father, I was making $55,000 a year. After I paid Santana and my car note, our insurance and cell phone bills, not to mention all the utilities, I barely had anything left to last me until the next payday. Good thing my father wasn't making me pay rent at his house.

The employees at the job were extremely ghetto and rude. At least once a day, one of the jealous bitches would call me a stuck-up bitch. When I told my supervisor, Manny, an older Hispanic man, he told me to deal with it on my own. The two who gave me the most problems were a fat chick named Mona, who had three kids to feed but she was worried about me, and an average-sized, plain-looking Jane named Keana, who had two kids. They were always talking shit about me and what made it harder was the fact that Mona and Keana were on my shift, so I had to work with them. The men who worked there were mad that I couldn't give them the time of day. Despite how they treated me, I never showed them that they were getting to me. I would come in with my head held high even though all I would hear were snickers from the booths next to me. I knew it was jealousy. It must have just killed them that they couldn't look like me, dress like me, and have a nice car like mine.

There was always a lot of tension when I went to work. Part of the reason they didn't like me was because I didn't associate with those bum bitches. In my opinion, they just weren't on my level. Both of them lived in the Carmelitos, located not too far from our work site. Their conversations always consisted of their kids and, of course, their different baby daddies, child support, and how many food stamps would be on their EBT card. I thought they were so pathetic and it wasn't my fault that I was better than them. I knew judging by their conversations that I made better decisions than they did. Also,

I actually had a man. Those miserable bitches didn't. And it wasn't my fault that I didn't grow up in the projects and my mother didn't have a case number. So work life was miserable for me. Even my days off were bad, Tuesday and Wednesday. I hated that. When I worked for my father I was off every weekend and could take an extra day if I wanted to.

And although things were good between Santana and me, I would be a liar if I said I was completely happy. I missed my friend Arianna and my family, minus my sister. By my not working for my father and not going to church, I felt completely alienated from my family. I wished they would stop being stubborn and my mother would accept the fact that I was staying with Santana. That's why I was surprised as hell to get a text from my friend Justin, saying he was back in town and that he wanted me to meet him at his favorite place for lunch: Roscoe's on the eastside of Long beach. Needless to say, I was super excited to see him. He said he wanted to fill me in on how the tour was and catch up with what was going on with me. I was super proud of him. So I agreed to meet him around one P.M.

My lunch break couldn't come fast enough. I hit the 710 Freeway and got to the Roscoe's in a good ten minutes. Justin was already there and seated, looking at a menu.

I rushed over to his table and he stood, laughing, looking as handsome as ever. Justin was tall, lanky, and dark-skinned. He wore skinny and neat dreads and had the prettiest smile.

"It's so good to see you!" I exclaimed.

"You too."

We sat down across from each other. "So how was the tour?"

He threw his head back laughed and clapped his hands. "A lot of fun. I love working for Trey Songz." He went on and talked excitedly about the tour, the different stars he saw, what it was like from state to state, the culture of the people, the food, the night life. It sounded very exciting.

"Congrats. No one deserves it more than you." I winked at him.

"Thank you, babes . . . So. The beautiful Alexis." He studied me for a minute before saying, "I invited Arianna to lunch too, but she refused to come. It confused me a little bit. And of course I heard about what happened with Dannon."

"A lot has gone on since you've gone, and as much as I love you, I really don't need your judgment or advice."

He used his index and middle finger like he was zipping his lips.

"I'm in love. His name is Santana. He is fine, sexy, manly, and he loves me. Dannon was all I had ever known as far as a man. You know that. But for some reason, Santana awakened and started something in me at the same time. It is hard to describe, but I fell for him hard. I haven't quite come down yet. It's like he put a spell on me, that, honestly, I don't want him to break."

The waitress came over and took our orders. I quickly looked at the menu and ordered Scoes Special #12. Justin ordered the same. We both ordered glasses of orange juice to go with our meal.

"I didn't think that Dannon would take the breakup so bad and would kill himself. But everyone wants to blame me for it. To be with Santana, I have to choose between him, and my family and friends."

"Well, you're my friend, I love you, and I don't know Santana to judge him or go by what people are saying. Lord knows I have my skeletons."

"What do you mean?"

He looked at me and took a deep breath. "I have something to tell you and I'm going to need *you not to judge me.* Because it's a big one. No one knows yet, not even Arianna."

The waitress came with our orange juice. I took a sip of mine and waited to see what he was going to say.

"What is it?" It couldn't be anything bad like what I was dealing with.

"I'm in love with a man."

My juice splattered from my mouth.

Justin threw back his head and laughed.

"Wait! Did I hear you right?"

"Yes, baby. I'm gay."

"How? When?" I asked this because Justin had dated girls when we were in school and even girls in the church.

"I have always known. But I couldn't tell you. We all grew up in the church. You know what the Bible says about homosexuality. So over the years, I tried to convince myself that I was just confused. But after the tour, I pretty much accepted that I am gay. I met a guy on tour. He's a drummer for several concert venues. Alexis, I feel like I'm in love with him. I don't know what my family will do to me if they find out. So please don't mention any of this."

"I'm not. I swear. I will take it to the grave. But what are you going to do?"

"I mean, I am just now accepting that I am gay. I have fought this for years. So for the time being, I'm going to keep it a secret until I feel I'm strong enough to handle it if my family, friends, and the church reject me. So right now, call me a punk, but I don't plan on telling them. I will live my regular life here and when I go back on tour, I will get to be with my babe. Like a secret love. But I had to share this with someone. I didn't tell Arianna because you know she can't hold water."

I laughed and the more I thought about it, he was going through the same thing I was. In order to be loved and accepted by his family he felt he couldn't be true to himself. I guessed I was stronger because I was able to be true to myself, that was for sure.

The waitress brought our food and we dug in. "Now tell me about this guy. What is his name?"

"Rahiem."

I smiled as his whole face lit up.

Then as we ate, he gave me the 411 on Rahiem. I was happy for my friend that he had found love. He also told me that he was looking into songwriting. He said being Trey Songz's backup singer allotted him other opportunities in the music business. I was also happy that I was at least able to preserve him as a friend and he would stay in my life. He assured me after our lunch date that we were friends forever.

Chapter 24

Justin called me on one of my days off and asked if I wanted to hear his demo. Since Santana was at school and I was home, bored, I said yes. I had nothing else to do but clean up and cook something for Santana. With my limited pocketbook, it was hard to keep making the gourmet meals I used to make. I could only do it a couple days a week and the other day shit was more basic, like meatloaf, mashed potatoes and gravy, or spaghetti. Santana often complained that I was losing my touch, and if it wasn't what he wanted he either picked at his plate or never finished it. But there was really nothing that I could do but keep applying for other jobs. The fact of the matter was, the economy was in a bad condition and there weren't many jobs out there. The inability to fix things often caused me to panic and fear I would lose him because I wasn't holding things down like I did before.

"Is taking care of me too much for you now?" he had demanded the night before.

"No." I did my best to give him some good head, although I was overworked, underpaid, and tired.

So when Justin offered to get me lunch from Claim Jumpers and bring it over, I jumped at the opportunity to order Santana filet mignon, a lobster tail, and a loaded baked potato.

"Only because I love you, will I get it," Justin joked. But I was sure he was expecting me to order a simple burger and fries or a sandwich and salad. And yeah, I ate a sandwich but it didn't come from Claim Jumper. I made a bologna sandwich with mustard and ate it well before Justin got there.

When Justin came with the food and chowed down on his tri tip sandwich with steak fries, I took my food and put it in the oven, saying I no longer had an appetite. He said nothing. No judgment, anything. That's why I loved him.

As he ate, I played his CD. His style reminded me of the singer Tank. Justin could give you R&B but go to church as well. He had an array of songs. There were three that were fast tempo, four moderate tempo, five slow, and two gospel songs.

"What do you think?" he asked me. By the time I listened to the CD he had already eaten, belched, used the bathroom, and was lying on his back on my sofa with his shoes kicked off.

I was impressed. "You know you sound good. You were going to church, boy."

He chuckled. "Thanks. You know what I was thinking. We could rerecord 'I'm Lost Without,' by BeBe & CeCe Winans. What do you think? You know you got the voice for it."

He stood to his feet and snatched me up. Playing around, he pretended he had a microphone. "'Day by day, no more reaction.'"

He held the imaginary mic to my mouth. "'You are my center attraction,'" I sang.

"See!" he exclaimed. "We sound good together." I laughed at his enthusiasm.

We continued to laugh and sing the song. He sang BeBe's part and I sang CeCe's. We were having a ball. It reminded me of when we used to sing together in church; that's when Santana walked into the living room.

He took one look at Justin's arm around my waist and scowled. I scooted away from Justin, walked up to Santana, and tried to kiss his lips but he turned his face away, so I only ended up kissing his cheek.

I turned back to Justin. "Justin, this is Santana. Santana, Justin."

"Hi. How are you doing?"

Santana gave a quick nod and walked into the room. I had hoped he would be friendlier to Justin. Justin didn't comment on it, which I was glad about. And I honestly felt a little embarrassed. But the good mood was pretty much ruined, Justin felt it. From the point of Santana being home, my thoughts were distracted by him; what he was doing, thinking, if he was talking to someone who it was and what he was discussing. So Justin said, to my relief, "Well, I need to get going." He stood and kissed me on my cheek. "So what are you singing?"

"Huh?"

"For your parent's anniversary party."

Shit. I had completely forgotten about it. It was usually a really big event where my parents got a DJ, had it catered, family, friends, and most of the members of my church came. I was always allowed to invite friends to it as well. Justin and Arianna along with their parents went every year.

Last year I sang "So Amazing" by Luther Vandross. Now with all the problems between my mother and family and friends I didn't even know if I was going to sing. Although I knew I couldn't miss it, I was in no mood to sing. I also knew that I could not bring Santana. *Maybe going would be an opportunity to mend things between my mother and father*. I didn't care if I ever saw my skank bitch of a sister, though, and if she was there, I wouldn't even acknowledge her.

"I'll wing it."

He laughed and walked toward the front door. I followed him. "That's one thing you can do, Alexis. Trust. With that voice of yours."

"Aww. So sweet."

Santana came out of the bedroom. He was on the phone. I heard him say, "Okay. Y'all on the way?" He walked right by us and went into the kitchen.

"It was nice meeting you," Justin called out to him.

Santana didn't respond.

"He probably didn't hear you," I lied.

He gave me another winning smile before walking out the door. I watched him leave.

"Aye. What the fuck I'm going to eat?" Santana yelled.

I walked into the kitchen and found him going through the fridge. "You in here entertaining niggas and shit." He slammed the fridge closed.

"It's not like that. That's—"

"Miss me with that shit! Where the fuck is dinner?"

I went to the oven, opened it, and grabbed the plastic container that held Santana's food. I put it in the microwave for two minutes. Once it was done, I set it in front of him. He ate it all while eying me with an evil look.

I wrung my hands, wondering if I should try to explain again who Justin was or if I should leave it alone so I didn't anger him further. I mean, the other day when we discussed how each other's days were, I told him I had lunch with an old friend and that it was Justin. I thought it would impress him if I told him that Justin had been away singing backup for Trey Songz. It didn't, but the point was I told him specifically who Justin was, so why was he tripping?

I decided to just leave it alone for the moment. If Santana brought it up, I would remind him that I had already spoken to him about Justin. If he didn't, he didn't. I would just chalk his behavior up to mere jealously. When Bria was living with us, there were several times that I had gotten jealous and had major attitude. In my jealous moments, Santana simply ignored me. And the thing was, our relationship, Justin's and mine, was completely harmless. Santana had my heart. He had a lock and grip on that shit that no one could break. He had to know that. So I left it alone.

A few minutes later, as I started on the laundry and was busy putting a load of clothes in the washer, I was surprised as hell to walk back into my living room and see Santana seated in the living room with three different girls. None of them looked familiar to me in the least and all were pretty and half naked, sitting on my couches.

Santana lit a rolled-up blunt and took a long drag before passing it around to the brown-skinned chick with a pair of lace leggings, a pair of cut-off jean shorts, and a half top, with some lace-up boots. Another girl had on a wife beater and a spandex skirt, the same type of boots as the other girl, and a hat. The other girl had on a pair of leggings and a half top like the other girl and the same fucking boots. This was how my sister dressed. *Why the fuck are they here?*

One girl was pouring herself a drink from a vodka bottle on the coffee table. "What you want to hear?" she asked Santana with *my* iPod in her hand.

"Put on that 2 Chainz shit. I fucks with that."

"*Hay*. That's my nigga too."

Then they all noticed me standing there. But none of them bothered to speak to me. I looked at them all like they were shit. And they looked at me right back with the same expression.

One of them said, "Who is this bitch?" I became a little fearful as she gave me a hostile look. I released the frown from my face.

I cleared my throat and said, "Santana." He looked my way, blew out smoke, but ignored me. One of the girls rushed over to him and opened her mouth so the smoke could go into her mouth.

I gasped and repeated, "Santana."

"Man, what?"

"Who are they?"

"The fuck you mean who are they? Why you questioning me? Didn't you have a nigga in here earlier?"

"That was different. He—"

"He had his motherfucking hands all over you! That's what made it different. You wanna have random niggas in our pad, I'll have random bitches in our pad. I wish you would say some shit."

"But—"

"Man. Shut the fuck up!" he yelled.

The chicks looked from me to him and busted up laughing at my humiliation. I wished if I knew they wouldn't fight me back, I could beat all of their asses. But they looked like some project whores who would hand my ass to me. So I resisted the urge.

I stood there like a prisoner. I didn't like the way they were now standing in my living room, now dancing in a sexy manner, grinding in front of my man. I didn't like the way he was watching them, licking his lips, his eyes raking up and down their curves. Staring longer in spots he shouldn't have: their breasts, hips, vajayjay, and asses as they popped it like they did it professionally. They seemed like they were strippers for hire. They were a fucking threat to me and I needed them out of my house.

"You had a nigga in here remember?"

I had to prove to Santana that it was nothing remotely similar to him having three sex kittens in my house. I had to. So before I could stop myself, I blurted, "Justin is gay," while flapping my arms to my sides. "So don't you see how this is different?'

He paused and looked at me.

I bit my bottom lip waiting to see the impact, hoping he would now feel bad and send the trash in my living room home.

I was shocked when he said, "I don't give a fuck. The way I see it, gay or not, if some pussy around, a nigga gonna hit on it. Miss me with that shit. Take your mothafucking ass in the room and think twice before you have a nigga all up in here!"

So that's what I did.

Chapter 25

As I sat in a corner of my parents' house during their anniversary party, over and over again guests stared at me. I knew they were perplexed as to how I could come so far and, in their eyes, sink so low. What they didn't understand or tried to ignore was that you can't control who you love, when love is going to find you, nor the magnitude of it. What I had experienced with Dannon was purely puppy love. But in the eyes of my family and friends, Dannon was the better man for me. It didn't really matter who they felt was better for me or if I felt that Dannon was better for me, because no matter what, I could not shake or rid myself of the love I had for Santana. At this point, with all the problems with my family and friends, and the hurt he had caused me, there for some reason was something that bound me to him. He was like a drug I couldn't kick. My thoughts were always floured with him, no matter how busy I was. I always wondered what he was doing, thinking, if he was thinking of me or missed me. I always ached to be back with him. This was something that I had never experienced before. My motives for life were to keep him by my side. For me, it had come to a point that it was at all costs. At least three different people from my church had come up to me that night and asked me, "Why? Why? Why?" But my reply was simply, "I love him. You can't control who you love." There were women who had married murderers who were going to be in prison for the rest of their lives and even on death row. Some of these women had never even met these men prior to their incarceration. Yet they remained faithful partners to them. There were women who agreed to share their husbands with five different other women who lived with them. They raised their children together. There were women who let their man beat them day and night and they didn't leave, and women who had allowed their man or husband to give them AIDS and they stayed. My point was simple: who you loved was who you loved and there was nothing more powerful than that. It was like that song by Kelly Rowland, called "Addicted":

> *I'm addicted to you*
> *When I see you*

Wanna be with you
Everything you do
All I dream of
When I wake up
My every thought is you.

That was how I felt about Santana. I loved him. No matter how many times he made me upset or did something to hurt me, the love just wouldn't leave . . . and the fact that I couldn't parade him in front of my family proudly made me feel bad. Granted, I know he had made some bad choices. But still . . .

When I was getting dressed to come to my parents' party, I felt bad. Here I was getting all pretty and he couldn't get handsome and party by my side. It sucked. He said he wasn't tripping, that he was going to throw back a couple drinks and watch a movie at home. So I had smiled sadly and left.

I had always had fun at my parents' party. Not so this year. I felt like an outcast. Arianna and a lot of the members of the church pretty much gave me the silent treatment. Although it bothered me, I told myself that since they wanted to be funny, they didn't deserve to be in my life anyway. My mother and father both seemed like they were in a good space. My mother looked beautiful and she partied the night away with her girlfriends. A couple times, she and my father danced together. The only one who really talked to me was Justin, and my daddy danced with me once. I was surprised that my mother didn't even bring up Santana, and, from the looks of things, my father didn't tell my mother I had stolen from him. I knew if he had, it didn't matter if we had Obama in the house, she would have brought it up. And it didn't appear that sweet, innocent Bria had told my mother that she had slept with Santana. I would have heard about that, too.

Justin came over and grabbed me just as "Cupid Shuffle" came on. "Come on, bestie. You know we can do at least one stepping song tonight."

I laughed and joined the others on the dance floor, finally for once that night having fun. It brought back memories of New Year's Eve. Every year my church had thrown a worship party and we always did all the stepping songs.

Justin and I laughed while doing the steps. My mother and father joined in the fun on the dance floor. But Arianna kept her distance. Bria was surprisingly missing. And I didn't inquire as to where she was because I didn't give two shits. Even some church members hit the floor. Then the DJ played some clean hip-hop songs like "Teach Me How To Dougie," which we started grooving to. I was having a blast and it felt good to push aside all those thoughts I was having prior to Justin grabbing me. He always had that ability. Even in school. That's why I loved him.

I was so into the music and the steps I was doing that I almost missed Santana coming into my parents' house, staggering like he couldn't stand on his feet.

He bumped into a table, causing people to look his way. Then he grooved his way over to the dance floor, yelling, "That's my shit!" He danced for a minute by himself and then yelled, "Play some motherfucking Too Short!" He started doing what looked like the Crip Walk. I knew it was the Crip Walk because I had seen Snoop Dogg do it in some of his videos. The people around him stopped dancing, and he was causing a big scene. I looked at my mother's disapproving expression, and my father refused to look his way. I was so embarrassed. He was pissy drunk. He continued to groove and even went so far as to take from his pocket a blunt, which he lit.

I tried to make my way over to him but he puffed on it, Crip Walked his way over to the DJ booth, and yelled, "Aye, nigga. Play some back-that-ass-up motherfucking music. Don't nobody want to hear that dry-ass shit!" He turned to people at the party and said, "Do y'all want to hear that shit?"

When no one responded he tossed a hand and said, "Fuck y'all."

"Santana!" I rushed up to him and grabbed his arms in mine, shaking him. I pleaded with my eyes before he said something else crazy. I put my finger to my lips.

"Hey, baby!" He struggled to stand up and tried to kiss me on my lips, but ended up kissing the air.

"You're drunk, Santana. What are you doing here?"

"Oh, I'm not invited? You don't want me here?"

"No. I—"

"Oh, y'all mothafuckas don't want me here huh?"

I looked at my mother and my daddy coming our way. "You need to leave," she said breathlessly to him.

"Why the fuck I gotta leave?"

"You were never invited. You are never ever welcome in my home!"

Santana tilted his head back. "Damn like that?" He turned and looked at my father, who had his head down.

"Yo. Bobby. I gotta leave, dawg?"

My father initially didn't answer.

Santana drunkenly tapped him on his shoulder. "Nigga, I'm talking to you! I gotta leave?"

"My wife wants you to leave so you gotta go."

"Nigga, I didn't ask about your wife. Fuck her."

"Santana, stop!" I yelled. My dad looked furious but it appeared that he was mentally trying to calm himself down.

"Move and shut the fuck up." He shoved me out of the way. "I asked you." He tapped my dad again. "You want me to leave?"

My father closed his eyes briefly and said, "Yes."

"Okay, nigga." He pulled his cell phone out of his pocket and fiddled with it. After a few seconds, he said, "*Mrs. VanCamp*. I got something to show you. It's an anniversary present."

A crowd formed around us. Justin stood nearby with his eyes wide.

"Look at this!" He shoved his cell phone in her face. Whatever he had on his phone had her so alarmed she had both palms of her hands on her face. But she wouldn't look away. Sound came in as Santana put his phone on speaker. Moans were heard.

My dad stood back as if defeated at this point.

"Santana. What did you show to my mother?"

My mom moaned in her throat, shoving Santana's hand, and ran off.

"You piece of shit." My dad tried to swing at Santana.

"Daddy, no!" I jumped in front of Santana, causing my father immediately to restrain himself or he would hit me. Justin came behind my father and grabbed one of my father's arms, telling him to calm down. My father snatched away, looked at Santana hatefully, and ran off, shouting my mother's name

This all caused the phone to fall to the floor. Santana struggled to stand, and laughed. "Happy anniversary. Fucking cat is out the bag, man."

I leaned down and grabbed the phone off the floor. I looked at the phone and gasped. My father was on the screen with a young girl and they were having sex.

"How the fuck could you?" was the look I gave Santana.

Santana wasn't paying me any attention; he then focused in on Justin. "What's up, cuz? I know you." Santana pointed at Justin. "You was at our crib the other day, man. Well, check this out pimpin'; you's one nigga I never have to worry about pushing up on or sniffing after my girl." He pointed at Justin again and said, "'Cause I know you don't get down like that. You into that freaky shit, sucking dick and getting fucked up your dook-shoot." Santana laughed loudly and repeated, louder, "Yeah! You like to get dug out, in your dook-shoot. A fucking flamer. So, nigga, you is welcome at my crib anytime. Gay niggas is welcome all day! Now if you was straight I'd have to shoot your ass for how you had your hands on my bitch."

I cringed as Santana spoke and didn't have the guts to look at Justin's face. I was terrified. His secret had gotten out and he had only shared it with me.

But when I got the guts up to look him in his eyes, the look he gave me was one I would never forget. He was so hurt. His lips trembled and his eyes locked with mine. Tears started sliding down my cheeks. My thoughts raced as to how I could fix this and I came up blank.

Chapter 26

I huffed out a deep breath, hesitating outside Justin's doorstep. I was trying to calm my nerves before I knocked and I still didn't know what I was going to say. How would I explain what I had done? He had trusted me with his deepest secret and I had betrayed him. *Damn*. I shook my head, highly disappointed in what I had done. Truth be told, it took me days to get over the whole situation. From Santana ruining my parents' anniversary party to humiliating Justin . . . I was so upset with him that I even considered packing his stuff and kicking him the hell out of my house. He'd been so drunk that night that when we'd gotten in the house, he passed out. . . .

I let him sleep only for the purpose of him sobering up. As soon as daylight hit, I was there with a glass of cold water, dousing him in his face.

He leaped up. "Baby! What the fuck are you doing?"

"*You should know, with the shit you pulled last night. I should be slapping the fuck out of you!*"

He looked confused. "*Man. I don't know what the fuck you talking about.*"

"*You ruined my parents' anniversary!*" I shoved him. "*And you ran your mouth and humiliated my best friend.*"

There was silence for a moment before he said, "*Babe. You going to have to fill me in because I was real fucked up last night. I was off that Mohawk.*"

I rehashed everything he said and did, down to showing the video of my father having sex with that girl. He looked amazed and buried his face in his hands. "*I'm sorry, baby. I swear to you, I would have never intentionally done something like that.*"

It was all a shock to me. I was still with questions that an apology just didn't cut. "*First off, what the fuck do you have to say about that video?*"

He took a deep breath. "*Man, that shit was before I ever met you. Before your pops put me on his payroll. I don't want to put your dad's business out there, but do you know how I met your father? The girl I used to fuck with, with the two kids, Reina? He was fucking her sister, Trish.*"

I thought back to what Spokeo had said. Another woman was living there. I shook my head.

"He used to come pick her up, take her out and shit, or they would go to a hotel, fuck, and then he would drop her off. Well, you know how some niggas can't see good pussy as what it is, good pussy, and leave it at that. Nigga started getting all sentimental and telling her all his business that she would share with Reina. She told her how he had bank, owned businesses and property, and how he was married. Trish and her sister were looking for a come up, plain and simple. They were some petty, broke-ass bitches. So Reina talked me into filming him having sex with her sister.

"The plan was for us to blackmail him into paying up and we wouldn't send the video to his wife and break up his happy home. He was getting closer and closer to her. He started stopping by, bringing Reina's kids gifts and shit. He brought grocery a couple times a month and paid the light bill. He didn't have to do any of that. And by me being there, kicking it with Reina, me and him started talking. The more I talked to him the more I started liking him as a person. He would come sometimes and just chop it up with me. Give me advice and shit. But

Trish was pressuring me to bust out the video on him. So one night I was about to and you know what the nigga did? He offered me a job. Me. He knew about my record and everything. And he was still willing to give me a chance.

"Aside from the fact that he was fucking another woman, he didn't like using condoms, and he was using some of his dough to buy her things and stuff for her kids who ain't his, I realized the nigga wasn't that bad. So I decided not to go through with the blackmail shit. That pissed them the fuck off. But I didn't care. In that short time, Mr. Vancamp had been more of a father figure than any other man in my life. I always told him I wouldn't go in his back yard if he stayed out of mine. He understood. That's why he always stayed out of my business with you. But I didn't think he ever thought you and I would have something."

Wow, *I thought.* My father has been cheating on my mother. *I was in shock. I mean, he was practically a man of the cloth. He was a deacon in our church. How could he do that to my mother? It was so foul. I didn't think I would be able to look at him the same way again. Judging from Reina, I was sure that her sister was just as much the piece of trash she was.*

"But I can't apologize enough for what I did last night, babe. I don't know what the fuck I was thinking pulling that shit out. I should have erased it." He shook his head bitterly. "And I shouldn't have said shit to your friend. I know you told me it was a secret."

That day Justin had come back over and those girls left. Things had calmed down between Santana and me and I told him never to mention what I had told him about Justin being gay. He said he never would.

"I hope you can forgive me for it. You don't get it, baby. You are the woman of a thousand men's dreams. I'm way out of my league with you. You are on a way higher level than me. You're beautiful, educated, and smart. I'm not good enough for you, baby." His eyes were watery and he started crying as he talked. "Sometimes I feel like I'm going to lose you to another man who's better than me. The thought of that drives me to drink."

His words made me soften and put things more into perspective. Santana felt threatened by what I was but he didn't need to. With his flaws and all, he was my everything. Without him, my future days would be gloomy. But yes. I was angry at what he did. The first few days it would be hard to forget it. But I knew I would *be able to forgive him because I loved him unconditionally. He was also inebriated. He would never have done it if he was sober.*

The day after the anniversary party, my father stopped by. When I answered the door and came face to face with him, it was one of the most awkward days I ever had with my father. I thought it was even more awkward than when my father had confronted me about stealing from him.

I said hello to my father. He didn't say it back. I cleared my throat and stepped back, inviting him inside.

"Is that sorry motherfucker in there?"

"Yes. Dad, I—"

He put his hand up, stopping me. "Listen. I don't want to hear it. I want him out of my house. You're my daughter so you're welcome to live here. But if you choose to stay with him you both need to be out and you have two weeks. You're my baby and I love you. I never failed you as a father. But I failed as a husband. My fear of my wife finding out that I cheated on her forced me to bite my tongue against a man I felt was no good for you. Well, it's out now. I want you to leave him alone. He is no good for you. I'm sorry that I wasn't strong enough to tell you before all this mess happened."

I looked at my dad and bit back tears. How could I tell him that, for once, I just couldn't obey him? I understood my dad being angry, but he had a responsibility here, too. I just didn't think that was the moment to throw it in his face.

"Dad," I whispered. "I love him, Daddy. You wouldn't understand. For me, nothing else matters without him in my life."

"Then I'm telling you this: I'm going to evict the both of you."

"Don't do this to me. I—"

"Two weeks! Or I'm evicting you both. I can't condone you being with that man. He is going to ruin your life. You're an adult, so I can't force you to leave him, but until you do don't expect my help or support."

He turned and walked down the porch steps.

"Dad!"

He stopped for a second as if it were a struggle to take another step. But he could never turn back around. I saw his shoulders shudder as he paused. Still, he walked on until he got to his car.

Suddenly I felt Santana standing behind me. His hands stroked up and down my arms. "I'm sorry, baby."

I turned and cried on his shoulder. It hurt me that my father wouldn't even listen to me. He was shutting me out because of my choice to stay with Santana. What if I shut him out of my life because he cheated on my mom? I knew Santana was wrong, but had my father never cheated there would be no video to show.

"Don't worry, baby. I got us in this situation. I will get us out of it."

I hoped he could, but I knew he couldn't repair my relationships with my father and Justin. His way of repairing was using $500 of his financial aid money to get us a one-bedroom unit in the Carmelitos. It was the last place I wanted to go. But there was no way I was going to be able to afford an apartment, both our car notes, insurance, cell phones, and utilities on my own. I mean I was given a raise and I was now making $1,500 a month, but it wasn't enough just yet. Santana said he would be done with school in another seven months and then he would get a job and help. So the Carmelitos was just a temporary thing.

Nothing was worse than leaving my job and trailing bitches at my job who hated me and following them into the Carmelitos, but what choice did I have? I would just have to weather the storm with my man until things got better.

I snapped out of my thoughts and knocked on Justin's door. I'd stopped by before going into work. It had been a month and a half since the party. I couldn't take it anymore. I had to see my friend. But as seconds flew by, I chickened out and started walking down the steps of his parents' home.

But, then, I hesitated on the third step when I heard the door open.

I turned around and came face to face with Justin.

The look he gave me was unlike any that he had ever given me. It was worse than how he looked at me at the party. It was filled with so much anger, as if I had just said every gay slur in the book to him. It was like he hated me. I knew I was responsible for this. I had betrayed his trust. It was different from the situation between Arianna and me. I felt no need to fix that one. She asked me to choose between her and Santana. Yes, he was wrong for throwing the drink in her face but he did it because she was getting in our business. Men don't like that. Whereas Justin accepted Santana with really no judgment. I needed to fix this. I needed to have at least one friend in my corner. My relationships with my sister, parents, and Arianna were estranged and irreparable. Justin was the last of the dying breed.

I pulled my lips in, waiting for him to speak. He didn't, he just stared at me.

"Hi," I said nervously.

He paused before saying, "What do you want?"

I jumped at the anger in his voice. "I know you're upset with me. But I wanted to tell you that I'm so sorry for hurting you, Justin."

"You think if you say sorry that makes it okay!" His lips were trembling and tears started sliding down his cheeks.

It killed me. I choked on a sob, trying to keep my composure. "I know it doesn't. I didn't mean to tell your secret."

"You betrayed my trust. You gave me your word. You have ruined my whole life. Nothing can change it. As for your apology, it means nothing to me."

"Justin. I love you. You are all I have left outside of Santana."

"This really isn't about *me*. You're only saying sorry because you don't have any more friends and your family has turned their backs on you because of your decisions. You are so selfish, Alexis."

"You're my best friend."

"Not anymore. I can't even show my face around town anymore. I can't go back to church, my father looks at me with disgust, and my mother can't seem to stop crying. I get called faggot every time I go out in public. This is all because of you. You are not my friend. You're nothing to me anymore." He yelled at the top of his lungs, "You're dead to me!"

I started bawling on his steps. His words cut me really deep. "Justin."

He was bawling too. "Get out of here!"

I placed a hand over my chest, aching at his hurtful words because I knew he meant every one of them. I backed off his steps, continuing to bawl. I stumbled on a step, lost my balance, and fell to the ground. I buried my face in my forearms.

He never attempted to help me. I heard his door slam shut and I was left there with his last words resonating in my ears . . . "You're dead to me."

Chapter 27

I didn't plan to bring up what happened with Justin to Santana. I wanted to keep it off my mind because every time I thought about it, it made me cry. And even if I did bring it up, I knew he couldn't do anything about it. I came home from work and walked into the kitchen, preparing to cook. But Santana had beat me to it, and was whipping something up.

"Hey, baby," he said.

"Hi."

"You okay?" he asked, stirring something in a pot.

I nodded.

"Cool. Go sit down. I'm going to bring you your food, babe. It's about time I start serving you."

I offered a smile, thinking, *how sweet*.

I went into the living room, which was furnished with all my things from my dad's place. We had been now living in the Carmelitos for over a month. Truthfully, it wasn't as bad as I

thought. I expected shootouts, excessive partying, rats, roaches, messed-up pipes. But it wasn't
any of that. And the place was actually really
clean. Still, it wasn't what I was used to. I was
told it took months to get into the Carmelitos.
But by Santana paying the $500 to a guy who
worked there, our application was expedited. I
knew it was crooked but whatever.

Our rent was only fifty bucks a month. The
reason it was so cheap was because they went by
Santana's income, which was only the $300 that
he got from General Relief. He also got $200 in
food stamps; that really helped. Santana kept
his $300 so he had spending money throughout
the month.

The only shameful part about living there
was seeing some of my coworkers. As humiliating as it was, I knew it was either live with him
in the projects or be without Santana and live in
my father's house. I told myself on a daily basis
that soon we would be able to move out and find
another place. Sometimes I did get discouraged;
with the economy being so bad, it was so hard to
find a job making more money. So I counted on
Santana to finish school so he could help me out
financially. When we first moved in, I wondered
if it made me look like less of a woman because
I wasn't giving him the life we had before. But

he said if anything, he loved and respected me more now because we were slumming and I was still holding it down like a down-ass chick. So it made me feel a lot better.

Santana came out of the kitchen, breaking my thoughts. He set a plate in my lap that had spaghetti, garlic bread, and salad. I nibbled on my food, not very hungry, as he slipped off my shoes and rubbed my feet.

"How was school?" I asked him.

"Good, babe. I learned how to work on carburetors. And did I tell you that once I graduate they're going to help me with job placement?"

"Oh, good."

He stared at me not really eating and asked, "What's wrong?"

"Nothing."

He continued to rub my feet. "I know what's wrong. You still bothered by that mess that happened with your parents huh?"

"No." A little part of me was still bothered by it. But my friend's words came back to me again and again as I sat on the couch. That was what was really on my mind, despite my trying to block it out. But I told Santana, "I'm just not hungry."

"Don't lie to me, baby," he said calmly. "Look, I know I've said this more than once but I am so sorry for what I did and the problems it caused. I love and respect your father. I never got a chance to love your mother because she refused to accept me. But I'm really trying to be a better man for you. I know you noticed I don't really drink anymore. Whenever I do, I fuck up like what happened with your sister. And I can't afford anymore fuckups."

He was right. Santana had laid off the alcohol. So I knew he was trying.

"If they would both be willing to talk to me, I would formally apologize to both of them. The same goes for your friend."

"Santana, I know you're sorry. Hopefully, one day my parents will be willing to listen to you. But for now, we just have to leave it alone."

"I know, babe."

"In all honesty, I'm a little unhappy."

He sat down next to me on the couch. "It will get better, baby. I'll be done with school soon, we can move, and hopefully with time passing, wounds can heal. Once they see me holding things down, maybe they will forgive me."

"Hopefully." I set the plate on the coffee table, got up, and walked upstairs to the bedroom. Once there, I stripped off my clothes and lay down on the bed. I felt really fatigued.

Santana came up and got into bed with me. He stroked my hair and said, "I don't like you upset, baby." He held me, and it did make me feel a little better. He had that comforting quality about him. "I love you, baby. I meant what I said when I told you I would give you the world. Don't leave me, baby."

I looked at him and smiled. "Santana. If you get a brain tumor they might as well put that tumor in me. Because there is no way I'm leaving you."

He smiled at that and held me tighter.

Call it stress, I guess, but the stress made me sleepy. So I fell asleep in his arms.

The next morning, I was alarmed when I went to the lot where my car was sitting on the concrete with no tires or rims on it.

I ran back to our apartment and banged on the door. "Santana!"

He rushed to the door in his boxers, no shirt on, with a toothbrush in his mouth. "What, baby?"

At this point my heart was pounding in my chest and I was crying. "Go look at my car!"

He ran out the door. I followed after him. Some of my neighbors had also stepped outside because of the commotion I was making.

I continued to cry loudly, feeling really violated. "We should have never moved in here!" I stormed away, hearing a few snickers, and someone said, "Aha. You stuck-up bitch!"

I ignored them, walked back into the house, and sat on the couch in anger. I knew I could not do anything about it and that calling the police was off limits. Santana had already warned me never to call them. He said that our house would be labeled the snitch house and we would be retaliated against for stuff that had nothing to do with us.

My cell phone beeped, telling me I had a new text message. When I checked it, I saw it was from my mother, saying she wanted to meet me when I was available. Although it felt good to hear from her, I was too pissed to respond at that moment.

Santana ended up taking me to work.

He parked and said, "I'll pick you up, babe."

I said nothing. I was too angry. I simply got out of the car and closed the door.

When I got inside my job, and reported to my booth, I was surprised that someone had put a brochure for Midas tires near my drawer. I heard laughter from Mona and Keana. Keana, who must have just gotten her weave done, kept flicking her hair over her shoulder and saying, "Dumb bitch."

I ignored her and grabbed my phone from my purse to turn it off. I saw my mom had texted me again, saying she needed to see me. I pressed the power button, shoved it back in my purse, and set the purse on the back of my chair. I ignored the snickers around me and tried to do my job the best that I could, despite my anger. The other bitch Mona walked by and purposely bumped my chair. When I looked at her she gave me a challenging look so I put my head down.

When it was time to go home, I had expected Santana to pick me up in his car, but instead, he was in mine.

"How did you—"

"I used my GR check. Come on, baby."

I smiled and hopped in. He had replaced the tires but I no longer had my expensive rims, or rims at all. But I guessed it was better than not being mobile. Although it was only for a short time, I didn't like being without my car. Since I was sixteen, I had always had reliable transportation.

Once I buckled up, Santana pulled out of the parking lot. I pulled out my cell phone and sent my mother a text, telling her I could meet for her lunch on Tuesday. My mother texted me back immediately, saying Tuesday was fine and instructing me to meet her at Eggs Etc in Long Beach, at 10:00 a.m. I was hoping that my mother was coming around, and if she was coming around, maybe my dad would too. Maybe they both would forgive Santana and I could move back into the house he kicked us out of.

When we got home, I saw that Santana had cooked again. This time he had made chicken wings with cream of mushroom soup, rice, green beans, and corn bread. It all tasted really good and I ate two platefuls. I was happy that Santana wasn't tripping about the fact that I was no longer cooking. Thing was, I got off work at 6:00 P.M. and he got out of school at three. It wasn't like it was when I worked for my dad where I made my own hours. Santana had taken it upon himself to start cooking our dinners. I was fine with it.

"Oh, you feeling better today?" he asked me, laughing as I threw down.

"Yeah." I didn't mention my mother because I didn't want to get his hopes up if the meeting wasn't successful. "I'm happy you were able to fix my car. Thank you, baby, for being so considerate."

"You my boo. What you expect?"

I blew him a kiss.

"Babe. You wanna stay up and watch a movie with me?"

I yawned and shook my head. Truthfully I did. But with my working longer hours at the job I noticed my energy level was far worse than it'd ever been. I slept a whole lot more than I used to. "No, baby. I'm going to go get some sleep." I got up, walked over to him, and kissed him. "Thank you for such a good dinner."

"I got some more dinner for you," he said, placing my hand on his penis.

I laughed. Normally, I would enjoy his love-making but I was too worn out tonight. But still I said, "I could always have more dinner."

"Naw, baby. You look like you can barely stand up. Go get some rest. Lethal can wait for you when you get your energy back up."

"You sure?"

"Yes, baby. Don't worry. I'm not going nowhere. I'm gonna watch this movie and I'll be up in a minute to cuddle."

"Okay, baby."

I took my hand away and went into the room to lie down. Before I drifted off, I hoped when I met my mother for lunch we could resolve all our issues.

Chapter 28

When I met my mother for breakfast, my stomach was in knots. I attributed it to my nerves. I noticed that my mother didn't look like the same vibrant mother she normally was. Her usually silky jet-black hair lacked the luster it normally had. She wore no makeup. She had bags under her eyes and she wore a simple sweat suit. She didn't have her nails done, and I couldn't remember a time where she hadn't had her nails done.

"Hi, Mom."

She tried to smile at me but she couldn't. It looked so tight. I looked away.

"There are some things I wanted to talk to you about, face to face. Things are chaotic at best right now. I don't know if your father told you, but we're getting a divorce."

Alarmed, I said, "Mom, no." I knew I wasn't a kid anymore, but the thought of my parents splitting up was very disturbing to me. It hurt.

I never ever thought I would hear the day they would divorce. I didn't want that. I wanted them to fix it and stay married.

"It's already done. I filed the papers already. He has already"—she stifled a sob—"he has already moved out."

I closed my eyes briefly, fighting back tears. I had always thought my parents had the perfect marriage, and they always seemed deeply in love. Growing up, I would watch them and hope my marriage could be strong like theirs. I felt my mother owed it to all the history they had to work it out.

"I don't know, Alexis. It seems like when he came into our lives, a black cloud hovered over us and our normal, happy life no longer existed."

I shook my head. I knew the "black cloud" she was referring to was Santana. But Santana didn't have anything to do with Daddy cheating. Still, I didn't want to go into defense mode so I simply listened.

"Your sister is in rehab."

I gasped. "What?"

"She had been in there for a while. When she came back home, after you kicked her out, she started stealing from us. It was only a matter of time before we found out that she was addicted to ecstasy."

So my sister's wild ways have finally caught up to her. I hoped my mother wasn't going to go in on Santana about this, too. I wasn't surprised that my sister had started messing with drugs. She was a wild child and she liked to play with fire.

"But I didn't come to talk to you about that. You remember when I told you someone was crank calling my phone? Playing porn in the background? Breathing heavy on the phone? Well, I finally got tired of it and went to the police station. They traced the calls." She swallowed hard before speaking again. "They said that the person responsible for the calls was Santana Marcelino."

My mouth shot open angrily. "Mom! Why would you sit here and lie like that?" Now she had made me angry. I knew she was going through stuff but it was outright pathetic to make something like this up! She was so determined to get me to leave Santana and the fact that she would stoop this low baffled me.

"This is why I didn't want to tell you. I knew in your little sick, twisted mind you would throw it back on *me*. What in the world happened to you? You have let this man brainwash you. I really don't know who you are anymore."

"And you know what, Mom? I can say the same about you. I'm sorry Dad fucked around on you! But that is not Santana's fault. And as for your precious Bria, even though you haven't said it, I know you are trying to blame Santana for that when we all know that Bria was a ticking time bomb. All her life, she has chased fire, and burnt you and Dad in the process. But you want to point the finger at someone, instead of evaluating whether *you* did the best parenting and set the proper boundaries for her!"

My mother's head snapped back at the last part. She looked really hurt that I attacked her parenting skills. And while I didn't want to hurt my mother, I was stating the truth. I mean, she didn't give a shit about hurting me by accusing Santana of crank calling her so why should I care?

I continued to talk. "Look, Mom. I love Santana. I have tried over and over to show you that he is not a bad guy. He loves me. Has he made mistakes? Yes! Has he owned up to them and made things right? Yes. He tried to right the wrong with you, but you won't let him. He needs to be perfect to get your approval. It's like no one is allowed to mess up with you except for Bria. She is allowed to be as imperfect as they come."

Tears slid down her face and she stared at me with a blank expression. She wiped them away and said in a low voice, "You are a lost cause."

That was enough. I grabbed my purse and stood to my feet. "Well, if you feel that way then stay the fuck out of my life."

I didn't even bother looking her way again. I walked away, frustrated as hell.

As I drove home I decided not to tell Santana about the conversation. All it would do was make him mad and probably make him feel like things would never get better between him and my mother. I would just have to hope and pray that one day they would.

I got another lovely surprise when I got up the next morning. I discovered that someone had keyed STUCK-UP BITCH on my car. Santana had already left and I was on my own. Once again people came out to the parking lot and watched me crying. My once beautiful car was now fucked up. And I didn't know what to do. So against Santana's wishes, I called the police. I waited for them to come, which was damn near an hour later, making me late as hell for work. Crazy part was, there was a police hub in the complex.

The cop walked over to me, taking his sweet little time. "What's the problem?"

"You don't see it? Someone vandalized my car!"

"Hey! Calm the fuck down."

I jumped at the sharpness in his voice and the fact that he had cursed at me. I had never had a cop speak to me that way. But I was in the projects: a place that, I was sure, cops looked down on. I was sure if he came over to where I used to live, he would have been nicer.

"Did you see the person who did it?"

I knew it had to be the two bitches from my job, Mona and Keana. "Stuck-up bitch" was their favorite tagline. So I said, "I know who did it. Two of my—"

He put a hand up, stopping my conversation. "Did you see them?"

"No."

"Then I really can't help you. I can take the report but unless it was witnessed, nothing can really be done." He jotted something down and handed a duplicate copy to me.

I was enraged but I knew I couldn't do anything about it. I tossed the paper on the ground, got in my car, and set out for work.

When I got there, luckily, my supervisor wasn't there. My eyes burned with fury as Mona and Keana continued to stare at me with smirks on their faces. This time I was brave and glared back at them. Normally the place was busy, giving me a distraction from their shit talking. But today we didn't have many customers and they continued to fuck with me.

"Damn! Move your chair up some," Mona's fat ass said. She shoved it and slid by to her booth.

I sucked my teeth and sighed deeply.

"What?" Her eyes were wide. "You act like you want to do something."

My heart sped up. I put my head down, fearful she would try to initiate a fight with me.

"That's what I thought, punk-ass bitch."

Then, not even five minutes later, Keana went in over me by saying, "Bitch act like she better than some fucking body but live in the same fucking projects that we do."

Mona added, "With her fucked-up car."

"Oooh." Keana put a hand over her mouth and started laughing.

That was it. I scribbled a note on a Post-it, saying I was feeling sick and needed to leave. I stuck it on my computer screen. Then I clocked out, grabbed my purse, and stormed out of there. I had to find another job.

I found two employment agencies; one was in Long Beach and the other one was in Lakewood. As I left the Lakewood agency, I drove past my old office on Candlewood. *Those were the good days,* I thought, *where I made good money, made my own hours, and had peace of mind.*

I had to get a job so I didn't have to be around those trifling bitches anymore. It needed to be a job making more money so we could move out of the Carmelitos. I even went to Work Source on Long Beach Boulevard, made a resume, and looked at the different job bulletins. I faxed my resume to several places. I tried to be positive about the job prospects, but there was so much competition, it was overwhelming. Still, I had hope something would come through. the ending of pretty much any book I have wrote

When I got home I was beat. Santana was home already and in the kitchen. "Hey, babe," he called.

I walked inside, kissed him, and said, "Check out my car."

"Huh?" He looked confused.

"Go see it."

"All right. Keep an eye on the meat."

I grabbed the fork from his hand and watched the steak he had in a frying pan with some butter, onion, and garlic cloves. It smelled good. But I was too stressed to have an appetite.

As I flipped the steak over, Santana walked back in the kitchen looking mad as hell. "When the fuck did that shit happen?"

"I saw it this morning. You probably didn't see it because it's on the left side of the car and you park on the right."

"Well, why didn't you call me, baby?"

"I called the police."

"Why the fuck you do that? I told you not to." He looked pissed that I didn't obey him.

"I wanted them to do something about it."

"Man, they ain't going to do shit. They don't care about no niggas living in the projects. Next time, do what your nigga tell you to do."

"Well, do something about this, Santana! I hate living here and I hate my job. Those bitches are always harassing me. And I know they are the ones who scratched up my car."

"Okay. I'm going to figure some shit out." He hugged me. "Let me deal with this, okay, baby? For now, just try to ignore those bitches." He started rubbing on my breasts, turning me on, and momentarily making me forget about the problems that I was having.

He laid me down on the kitchen floor, unbuttoned my dress, and pulled it apart. He slid up my bra and started licking on my nipples. I moaned and bit my lip when he pushed my panties aside and started rubbing on my clit. I was getting so turned on that I wanted Santana's dick inside of me. I sat up and grabbed it, feeling his thickness between my hands instantly harden. He picked me up off the floor and sat me on the counter. Santana then ripped off my panties and inserted his dick inside of me. I screeched as his thickness widened my opening. He completely filled me and pumped fiercely.

"Damn, Santana!" He took it out and started eating my pussy.

I squirmed and moaned as the budding pleasure inside of my pussy threatened to explode. He licked up and down my shaft and let the tip of his tongue flicker on my clit.

"Santana, please." My legs started shaking.

He yanked me down off the counter, turned me around, bent me over, and started fucking me in my ass. The shit felt so good because as he fucked me in my ass, he fingered my clit. I nutted and nutted and nutted. By the time my baby finally busted, I was feeling so good and so weak, I slid to the floor. He simply scooped me up and carried me upstairs for round two. I sucked his dick, got it back hard, and rode him hard and fast into the night. Dinner was forgotten by both of us.

Chapter 29

The night of lovemaking made my mood a little better when I went to work the next day. I was surprised to see my manager standing near my work booth. Mona and Keana both looked at me and smirked when I walked past their booths.

"Alexis, I need to talk to you."

"Okay." I followed him to his office. He sat down and I sat across from him.

"I understand you abandoned your post yesterday."

"Yes. But I left a note."

"It doesn't matter. I wasn't here to excuse you home and wasn't aware that you had left until I came in today. And, more importantly, you left your drawer open. That was so stupid of you."

He opened my employee file and pointed to my signature on one of the documents lying on top of the stack of papers. "When you signed on as an employee, you signed this document, stating that you would not abandon your post and you wouldn't leave your drawer open."

"I know, but—"

"But what?"

"It slipped my mind. I'm dealing with a lot of issues right now and what doesn't help is being constantly harassed by Mona and Keana. I told you about them before and you did nothing."

"Maybe if you had made an effort to be nice to the other employees instead of walking around with your nose in the air you wouldn't have had the problems you have. But the bottom line is *you* left your drawer open. There is no second chance to do that again. I'm going to have to let you go."

I gasped. "What? Just like that? Without a second chance?"

"Your problem is that you have only worked for your father. You haven't experienced the real world yet. I don't give second chances here. Go back to him for a second chance." He slid an envelope to me. "That is your last check."

I stared down at the envelope and couldn't believe he was firing me. No second chance or anything. And the look on his face told me that he was serious and that was his final decision.

I stood, grabbed my paycheck, and angrily said, "Well, fuck you." I shoved the papers off his desk and stormed out of his office.

I went over to my booth and grabbed the two framed pictures of Santana and me, and walked past Mona and Keana.

They both laughed. Keana said, "Bye, bitch."

As I walked past them I said, "Fuck you, bitches! You both not shit and don't have shit!"

The manager came out and shouted, "Get out of here!"

They both laughed at that. It was humiliating so I rushed out, trying not to let them see me cry. Once I got in my car I punched off, still crying and wondering what I was going to do. I was now unemployed. How was I going to be able to pay all the bills now?

I took my last paycheck and paid all the bills, including the rent. But that left me with virtually nothing.

I called my father, hoping he would loan me a couple thousand dollars to hold me over until I got another job. He asked me if I was still with Santana. When I said yes all I heard was the dial tone. I threw my phone in anger.

I was so stressed that when Santana walked in the door, I was sitting on the couch in tears rocking back and forth.

"Babe. What's wrong now?"

"I lost my job, Santana."

"Man, fuck!" He sat down across from me.

"I don't know what to do, Santana. I can keep looking for a job, but there really is nothing out here right now because of the recession."

"I can try to get a job, Alexis. I know I won't make much and I will have to drop out of school, but fuck it."

"No. I don't want you to drop out of school, Santana."

"Well, shit, I gotta do something, baby. We gotta eat. We gotta pay these bills somehow. I can always go back to work for those Jamaicans."

"Santana, are you crazy? No."

"I'm the nigga. I have to think of something. You don't want to live in the Carmelitos no more. They fucked up your car. Shit! Man, this is frustrating! And I hate how you always unhappy." He stood to his feet.

"Wait! Where are you going?"

"I'm going to try to make some money. Buy some dope to sell or something. Do a lick."

"No." I stood and ran in front of him, trying to block him from leaving. I didn't want him to go out and do anything stupid that would land him in jail or dead. He simply shoved me out of the way and went out the door, despite me yelling his name and begging him to come back.

***

Despite the fact that I blew up Santana's phone, he wouldn't respond. I cried and threw things out of frustration. I continued to call and constantly peeked my head out the door to see if he had come back. I wished I hadn't been so upset about losing my job. I should have lied and said I had other prospects. I had stressed him to the point where he felt he had to go out and do something stupid. I wrung my hands together and called his number again. He didn't answer. It had been about four hours since he had left.

I looked outside again and saw him pull up.

I ran outside toward him and waited for him to get out of his car, with my arms crossed under my breasts. Once he did, I punched him in his chest. "I told you not to leave!"

"Stop, baby."

I shoved him. "Don't you understand that I love you! I would kill myself if something happened to you."

He opened his arms for me to slip in them. But I shook my head and backed away.

"Calm down. I didn't do shit. I just went for a drive. Come on. Let's go inside and talk."

I obeyed and followed him.

Chapter 30

"Look, babe. I know how you feel about me doing anything illegal. But right now, let's face the facts. We are in a bad position. And we got to do something about it. Before you start frowning your face, just listen."

I tried to relax.

"*We* can come up off a few licks."

"Licks?"

"Yeah. Licks. Where you rob someone."

"Santana—"

"Shut the fuck up. Damn! Listen to me first."

I clamped my mouth closed.

"Babe. It's not what you think. We can just do it for a little while until we get up enough money to move and enough money to get us by the next couple a months. We gonna at least need two Gs to move and at least some thousands put away to pay our bills until you get a job. And then when I finish school, we Gucci. We good. Listen. I know a nigga, he lives in LA. He got

the hookup with the DMV. You bring him a hot
car he will give you seven Gs for it. Ten Gs if it's
something like a Benz, BMW, or Escalade. They
know how to change the VINs and shit so the car
is not traceable. All we got to do it get you dolled
up, go to a bar, scope out a sucka-ass nigga who
got pussy on the brain. Like a square-ass nigga.
You can act like you selling pussy. Tell him your
price. Go get in the car with him, ride to the
motel. I will trail you guys. Then when you go
in the room, I'll bust in with a gun, take his keys,
and we out. When I get them, you can bounce
with me."

"What if the guy calls the police on us?"

"I thought about that. The targets have to be
married men who got something to lose. I'll
scare his ass. Take his license plate, threaten to
pay his wife a visit. He won't call the police on
us. And we will only do this a few times until we
get up the money we need. Then we can move
the fuck up out of here to a nice place; we can
even get your car fixed and put some away. How
it sound, baby?"

Really it didn't sound too bad. No one was getting hurt and he was merely taking the person's
car. My only fear about the whole scheme was
being in the room with the guy until Santana
got there.

He saw my hesitation, so he said, "You can have a gun for a precaution. But, babe, as soon as y'all get in the room I'm busting in with a gun to scare his ass. And we'll just make sure the tricks we pick are chumps, for added protection. Don't trip, baby, I got you. You know I'm never going to let anything happen to you. You trust me?"

I looked into his convincing eyes, took a deep breath, and thought about how fucked up my car was and the hell I had experienced with those two bitches. I didn't want any more of that. I wanted peace of mind and to enjoy my days without stressing about the people I had to work with. And, like Santana said, we would only do this a couple times.

"Okay. Let's do it."

He got on his knees, crawled over to me, and kissed my lips.

We decided to do the scam in Newport Beach because it was far away from home. I questioned my chances in a white bar. But Santana said that as pretty as I was, I shouldn't have a problem snagging someone. He also said that a lot of white man secretly wanted to bed a sista. I knew that Newport was where very wealthy people lived. The parking lot was filled with luxury and designer cars.

We went to Duke's Place, on West Coast Highway. I replayed the steps in my head over and over again as I settled at the bar with a skin-tight dress and heels. I ordered a Midori Sour. I had on heavy makeup and my hair was flat ironed, so it hung silkily around my shoulders and down my back.

Step one: look around for someone showing interest. Give him continuous eye contact. If they come over and offer to buy me a drink, I am to be super witty and charming, willing to buy them a drink. Show my thighs and keep my chest pushed out. Continue to engage them in a conversation. Step two: if they bite and make a move on me, offer my services to them and give them a very reasonable quote. Forty for head, seventy for sex, and one hundred for both. Step three: leave with him in his car. Continue to talk to him in the car to keep him distracted and he doesn't notice he is being trailed. Step four: go into the room, start stripping down.

There were plenty of men who were giving me the eye. But the one I kept my eyes on was a thin-looking white man who was shorter than me and didn't look like much of a threat. He was sitting three seats down from me and his eyes continued to float over to my way. Then he would fearfully look away. I didn't. Every time he looked my way, he saw that my eyes were still on him and I gave him a pretty smile. Finally, after a couple minutes, he made his way over to where I was.

"Hey."

"How are you doing?" I asked.

"Pretty good. Now that I'm talking to a pretty lady like yourself."

I blushed. "That was so sweet, thanks."

"Tim."

"Lola."

"What are you drinking?"

"Midori Sour." I had just finished mine.

He bought me another. I sipped on it while he drilled me. "So did you come here alone?"

That's when I remembered to check and make sure he had a wedding ring. He did. *Shame on him.* "Yep. How about you?"

"Yeah. Wanted to get out of the house. I didn't want to hear my wife's mouth tonight. Our two kids are bouncing off the walls. No one seems to understand that sometimes I need a break too."

"Trust me, honey, if anybody understands it's me." My right hand rubbed against his as it rested on the counter. I gave him a sexy look, hoping I was convincing him.

He paused and stared at me for a moment as if he was shocked I was even talking to him.

"So. What do you do?" I asked. I took a sip of my drink, and my other, free hand kept rubbing his hand on the counter.

"I flip houses."

"Oh, really . . ." I stopped myself before I blurted out my personal business about my dad owning property. "That's impressive."

"So what about you?"

I chuckled, making him laugh as well. "Let's just say I'm in the people-pleasing business."

His brows furrowed together. Then he laughed and shook his head. "And all this time I thought it was because you were really interested in me. I mean you're beautiful. I know I'm not much of a looker. So I should have known there was a catch."

I laughed. "Everything costs, right?"

Without hesitation he said, "How much?"

I recited, "Forty for head, seventy for sex, and a hundred for both."

He nodded and looked around before turning back to me. "When you looking to get out of here?"

"When you looking to get out of here?"

"Meet me outside in five minutes."

True to Santana's words, the shit was so damn simple. I kept him engaged in his car, which was a black Audi. I talked nonstop in the car. I told him that I was a singer and I even belted out an Alicia Keys song.

"Wow," he said, looking at me as he drove. "You have a beautiful voice."

"Thank you."

"Amazing," he said. He pulled into a motel that was a few minutes from the bar.

"How about you? Do you have any hidden talents?"

"Nope, not really. I never had any type of artistic talent. I've just always been good with money." As he spoke I looked in the rearview mirror. Santana told me he wasn't going to be directly behind the car.

"Well, that's definitely a talent!"

He laughed, parked, and got out of the car. "Be right back."

I waited in the car as he went and paid for the room. When he came back to the car with a hotel key, I swallowed hard and got out of the car. His hands continued to rub up and down my butt as I followed him to the room.

I discreetly looked behind me for Santana as he unlocked the door. I saw his car parked and his headlights off.

We went into the room. He tried to hold the door open for me, but slyly, I bent over and pretended I was fixing my shoe and said, "Go ahead." He did and I went in last. This was deliberate so I could make sure the door was kept unlocked for Santana.

He wasn't paying any attention; he was too busy making sure the curtains were closed.

Then he turned to me, smiled, and said, "First things first." He reached in his wallet and handed some money to me.

"Thank you." I slowly counted it and put it in my purse.

He started unbuttoning his shirt. He had managed to get his shirt off, when Santana came busting through the door.

The guy jumped.

"Aye, my man. You don't want to get hurt. Just give me your car keys, money, and you good."

His eyes were as wide as saucers. Before he could stop himself, he peed. I looked away, embarrassed.

Santana shook his head. "Give it up."

Without hesitation, he gave his wallet and car keys to Santana.

Santana smiled menacingly at the man, pulled out his driver's license, and showed it to the man. "You call the police and trust and believe someone will be paying you a visit real soon." He looked at Tim's left hand. "Oh, and you married."

"With kids," I added.

He looked at me, surprised. "You set me up?" he demanded.

"Shut the fuck up," Santana said. "Come on, baby." Santana walked backward, keeping his eyes on the guy. I gave the guy one last look before rushing out of the room.

I didn't breathe a sigh of relief until we dropped off the car and Santana hopped in the passenger seat of his car (because he drove Tim's car and I drove his) and we were on the way home, $10,000 richer.

Chapter 31

These "licks" were super easy. And, in all honesty, since the men we planned to hit up had money, I didn't feel so bad stealing a car from them. Our plan was to do four more licks and be done.

We always waited a day in between doing our next one and used that day to figure out what spot we were going to hit up next. I suggested that we do the city of Brentwood and Santana was with it. People out there had money and it was a distance from where we lived and our last setup.

This time, we went to 760 Cigar Lounge. With the place being filled with busty blondes I didn't think I was going to have any luck there. In fact, after waiting for forty-five minutes and not really getting any attention from anyone I decided that it was best to pick another spot before it got too late. But as I made it to the exit, brushing past several people, someone curved an arm around my waist and said, "You're not leaving. I just got here."

I turned and looked at a tall, lanky-looking blond guy. He had sparkling blue eyes and was handsome. He was a few inches taller than I was. I wagered Santana would be okay with him. And plus we both carried guns. But I knew with how skillful we acted and how well we had planned this I would not ever have to pull out my gun.

I chuckled. "Well then, handsome, I guess I'm not leaving."

He gripped my hand in his and walked me over to the bar. He pulled the stool out for me and I sat down. He sat down as well.

"So what's your price?"

"Excuse me?" I was taken aback by how bold he was to assume I was a prostitute.

He chuckled. "Come on. You know what I mean. Why else would you be in here?"

Now that racist-ass comment pissed me the fuck off. I was happy we were jacking his ass. "Forty for head. Seventy for sex, and one hundred for it all," I said tartly.

"Let's go."

As cocky as he was, I expected him to be in a damn Phantom. But he instead had a Porsche. I slipped inside and as soon as he started driving, I tried to start a conversation.

"So what do you do?" I asked him.

He ignored me and weaved through traffic. I looked in the mirror to make sure Santana was close. He was.

"Well?" I asked him, chuckling.

"Do me a favor. Shut the fuck up. I'm not paying you to talk," he said causally, like he'd said to pass the butter.

I was pissed but I had to go through with this. But when that gun was in his face and he peed on himself like Tim had done I was going to laugh in his face.

We pulled into a seedy-looking motel called El Dorado. I waited for him to get the room. He was so distrusting he took his keys out of the ignition and walked to the office to get a room.

I spied Santana, parked.

He came back to the car, so I got out and followed him to the room. Since he didn't bother to let me go in first I didn't have to worry about playing it off. He walked in and I walked in after him.

I stood in the center of the room.

He turned around, looked at me, and said, "Well, what are you waiting for? Take off your fucking clothes."

"Can I have—"

"You'll get the fucking money when I'm done."

The bastard was so damn rude. I couldn't wait for Santana to come in the room.

He starting stripping down. I reached for a button on my shirt as I watched him. Damn, where was Santana?

Once he was nude, he placed his clothes on a corner of the bed and sat down.

I worked my way down all my buttons until they were all undone. I took it off and still, Santana wasn't in the room. I started to panic, thinking I was going to have to get nude in front of this man because he was taking so long.

"Let me see your ass," he ordered as I unzipped my skirt. I turned so my back was to him. I bent over and put my butt in the air and heard his sharp intake of breath.

"Now take it off." I strategically stayed with my back to him and reached for my spandex skirt's zipper. At this point, I figured I could get things started, then hopefully Santana could come in. I mean I had the gun; so what if I was a woman? I held the power. Although I would never fire it.

While tugging down the skirt with one hand with my free hand I reached in my purse for the gun. I pulled it out, spun around, and pointed it at him. "Give me your keys and wallet."

He gave me an evil look. Man, if looks could kill. "Bitch! So this was a setup?"

"Shut up!" I looked behind me quickly to see if Santana was going to come walking into the door. Still nothing.

"I can't wait for my man to come in the door and fuck your ass up, *bitch!*"

"I can't wait either." His voice was steady while mine was shaky. "Give me the fucking keys like I said, and your wallet."

He pulled his clothes toward him and reached in his pocket saying, "I hate ghetto scum like you. A typical nigger."

His words enraged me. "Shut up!" I yelled. I pulled the safety like Santana had taught me and continuing to aim the gun at him. Damn, where was Santana?

He got scared all of a sudden, by the sound of the safety.

"Okay. Relax. All I wanted to do was have a good time with you. I had never been with a colored chick before."

I shook my head at him.

He eased the wallet out first and held it up.

"Put it by my feet," I ordered.

He obliged. I bent down to retrieve it, all the while holding the gun on him.

I stood up. "Now toss the keys near my feet."

"Okay. Whatever you say. I don't want you to kill me or anything." His tone was so sarcastic.

"Just do it! Stop fucking talkin'—"

In a flash, he tossed the keys toward my face. I jumped back to avoid getting hit in the face, and that was when he took a leap toward me. In the millisecond that he leaped toward me, I made the worst choice I could have ever made. It was a choice I made without thinking. It was pure panic, and in that pure panic I fired the gun.

The bullet hit him in his chest and his pale skin instantly was covered with blood.

He collapsed to the floor.

I gasped and dropped the gun.

I watched his body continue to shudder and his breathing become ragged. I walked over to him filled with complete dread and shock. I had shot him and still no Santana. *Please, God,* I prayed silently. *Don't let this man die.*

I reached for the phone and dialed 911.

When they answered I said simply, in a bit of a shock, "I shot a man."

Chapter 32

Two Months Later . . .

Dear Santana,
If you are alive I need to hear from you! Babe, you have no idea how much I miss and need you. Jail is no joke. Do you know that some of the chicks in here are so jealous of me that they jumped me in the shower and used a shank to cut off all my hair! Crazy huh? The thing I'm wondering is what did they plan on doing with the hair? But after about ten ass whippings, I started fighting back and now they leave me alone. They found out I could sing. Now, every time I turn around someone is asking me to sing a tune for them. Of course, at least once a day I sing our song, "Excuse me." But seriously now, I don't know what happened to you that night. If this is about the case you don't have to hide out anymore. You didn't pull

the trigger, I did. And I am the one who got life in prison for it. I'm sure you didn't want to be held accountable for any of it. But it's over now. Santana, I desperately need to see you and for you to start writing me. I love you so much. I always said that you are my everything. And without hearing from you, baby, my days are so gloomy. Now I don't know where you are. But I'm going to give this letter to my mother. She is going to visit me today. Would you believe that my sister, Arianna, and even Justin have all come to see me? They all forgave me. That makes me so happy. I just wish it were under other circumstances. I wish I were free. Sometimes when we go outside for rec, the birds fly over my head and I just watch them and smile. I close my eyes and pretend that I'm one of them and able to fly out of this place. But in all honesty, when I open my eyes and I see the birds are gone, I realize that my freedom is too. There is nothing I can do about it. At first I tried to take my life by hanging myself. But it didn't work. A CO found me just before I went out completely. So now I just have to keep on moving forward. Well, I have to go. Visiting is soon. Please, please, please respond. I love you always,

*   Alexis*

*PS: Please, please, please write me,
Santana!*

I folded the letter and placed it in an envelope.
So much had transpired in the last two months.
For starters, I was charged with first-degree
murder. Yes, he died from that one gunshot.
Turns out the bullet penetrated his ribcage and
entered his heart. What luck I had. His parents
were so enraged they wanted the death penalty.
So did the DA, and that was what they asked
for. Nothing felt worse than being arrested and
sent to jail. Never in my wildest dreams did I
think this would happen to me. Not a twenty-
four-year-old college graduate, with the world
at her feet that went down in a blaze. I was on
various news stations and the world seemed to
be baffled as to how I could be in that position.

My parents, thank God, hired a lawyer, but in
all honesty it just never looked good. I mean I
had killed an unarmed man who I was there to
rob. Often, I wished I could turn back time and
never listen to Santana when he told me about
this scheme. If I really loved him and he really
loved me we should have both found another
way to get by without doing illegal things. I, to
this day, don't know what happened to Santana.
I don't know if he is in jail, dead, or if he ran
off. Did I blame him for my predicament? No,

because I was just as much a part of the incident as he was. And I made the dumb choice to go through with the plan when Santana disappeared. I could have walked away. I had the gun after all. I could have left. My lawyer tried to argue that I was a good kid, from a good family, who had never been in trouble with the law. He told the court that I never planned to go to that hotel and to kill that man, and that I acted out of panic and felt my life was in danger.

The day of the final ruling, the judge gave it to me. My parents, sister, Justin, Arianna, and even members of my church were there. They had done so many barbeques and praying events for my freedom it was crazy.

The courtroom was super quiet when the judge spoke. "While the jurors will make the final verdict, I will say this, Ms. Vancamp. You should be ashamed of the poor choices you made. You have the whole world talking about you, scratching their heads, trying to figure out how someone with the opportunity you had would blow it. And while you may not have gone to that hotel that night to commit murder, murder is in fact what you did. You went to the hotel with the intent to rob that man. Had you not made the choice to do that, you probably wouldn't be standing in my courtroom today."

He cleared his throat. "Jurors, do you have your verdict?"

One of the jurors, a young Hispanic girl who looked around my age, stood and said,

"We, the jurors, find the defendant, Alexis Vancamp, guilty of first-degree murder and sentenced to twenty years to life, without the possibility of parole."

I heard my mother scream at the top of her lungs. I collapsed on the floor, literally under the table. It took for the CO and my lawyer to get me to a standing position. But as they had me standing, the room started spinning and I passed out.

I was in denial for a long time after my sentencing. I didn't bother eating or even get out of my bed. I was suicidal and wanted to die. But after my suicide attempt, I accepted that this was my fate.

"Vancamp, let's go. Step out."

I snapped out of my thoughts, grabbed my letter, stepped out of my cell, and followed the guard to the visiting area.

I saw my mother sitting at a table. I was happy that I was no longer at Twin Towers because visiting was always behind a glass window. Here, we were able to hug each other and hold hands at Women's Valley State Prison.

As I walked, I smoothed my short hair back and walked over to my mother with the letter in my hand. My mother's eyes were watery as she saw me.

"Hey, Mom." I gave her a hug.

She felt like skin and bones and looked that way, too. "What happened to your hair?"

"Aww. Nothing, Mom. I cut it off. It was too much trouble, keeping it up in here." I lied because I didn't want to stress my mother out more. "So are you back at work?"

"I'm still on my leave of absence."

"Oh, okay. How is everyone?"

"You need to ask?" she managed to choke out. She looked at me like she was so heartbroken. It made me feel bad. I knew I had greatly disappointed her. But all that I did, I did for the love of a man. So that we could survive together.

"Mom, I was wondering if you could do me a big favor."

"I put money on your books, so—"

"No, Mom. It's not about that. It's about . . ." I cleared my throat. "It's about Santana."

"Wait a minute. After all that he has done, from leaving you that night, to dropping off the face of the earth, you have the nerve to mention that man's name. You have ruined your own life on account of that man!"

"Mom, see? That's the thing you never understood. Everything I did for and with him was because I wanted to. Am I mad he disappeared that night? Yes. But for all I know, he could be dead somewhere; he could be in jail. He wouldn't have just left me, Mom. Don't you get it? My love for him is forever. It's not going anywhere and I know he feels the same."

"Stop it, Alexis! Just stop it about that man."

"Mom. I'll stop when I find out where he is. I know I asked you before and you denied me because your focus was on my case and all, but, Mom, I really need you to go over to the Carmelitos and see if he is there or if anyone has seen him. If what you feel is true, that he is deliberately ignoring me, and he tells me himself, then and only then will I let this go."

"Alexis!" She put a hand to her chest and lowered her voice. "You have to stop it. You have to let this go," she told me calmly.

"I love him. Don't you get it?"

"He is not dead, okay? He is not in jail."

Thank God, I thought, crying happy tears. "How do you know, Mom? Then where is he? Can you take the letter to him?" I shoved it near her hands on the table.

"You can't see that man again. You can't love that man, understood?"

Here she goes again. "Mom, why are you—"

"He's your brother!"

I looked at my mother, confused. "Mom? What are you talking about?"

She slid a folded-up piece of lined paper toward me. I unfolded it and immediately recognized Santana's handwriting on it:

Yeah, you punk-ass bitch! You thought you were just going to go through life living well after the mistake you called yourself getting rid of twenty-nine years ago? I like how you had that clause in your adoption, that you didn't want to be contacted by me should I ever grow up and want to know who my real mother is. And you have the nerve to be a fucking social worker? That was some cold shit. All I ever wanted was to see what it felt like to have my mother's love. My birth certificate said my father is unknown. You were such a fucking tramp-ass bitch that you don't even know who you got pregnant by. So as soon as I hit eighteen, I took my first Yokum check and hired a PI to find your ass.

Do you know all the suffering that I had to go through because you couldn't just have kept me and loved me? I have been abused and given the fuck away. You were my mother. You were supposed to love me, take care of me, make sure I didn't get hurt like you did for those spoiled bitches. Well, looks like they're hurt now. That dumb bitch Alexis actually thought I loved her when this was all a setup from the very beginning. The plan was to ruin what you loved most: your precious daughters. Originally, I wasn't going to fuck with Bria. I wanted the bitch who took my spot as the oldest, and her dumb ass was putty in my hands. So my plan was called the Demise of Alexis Vancamp. I brainwashed her from day one. I lied about myself having a fiancée. Man, I set her ass up over and over again. But then, when Bria moved in, I figured, why not ruin her life too? But who knew it would be so easy? Who knew that Alexis would be so dumb and become so in love with me? She got herself in some hot water when she killed that innocent man. I just thought she would end up raped or beat up or some shit like that by her going to a racist spot. I didn't think her scary, punk ass would ever pull the trigger of a gun, much less bust a grape in a fruit fight. So her life is over. She might as well kill herself. And as for your other little bitch, she will be an addict for the rest of her fucking life. She will never be able to live like a normal person. I don't

care how many times you put her in rehab.
I give her six more months, she will be on
Fig, selling her pussy. And that's what you
get, bitch. I hope you cry every day for the
rest of your life! I hope your future days
are dark and lonely like my years were
because my mother didn't love me enough
to just keep me. Matter of fact, I hope you
kill yourself, bitch! Meet your demise with
your daughters.
   Yours truly,
   Santana Marcelino

I gasped as the letter dropped from my hands
and floated to the ground. Horrified, I looked at
my mother.

"I'm so sorry, baby. I didn't know until I got
this letter last week. Years ago, I was in college
and I found out I was pregnant from a one-
night stand. My parents were very religious. My
father was a deacon and I decided it was best to
give the baby up because they didn't believe in
abortion and . . ."

I stopped listening. All this was a lie? The love
we shared, it was all a lie? I did this all for nothing? And now I had lost my whole life behind it.
I would rot away in prison. Santana never loved
me. He used me to hurt our mother.

I stood and clawed at my face, screaming at the top of my lungs. All this time I had been sleeping with my brother.

"Baby, don't." I closed my eyes to my mother. She pulled my hands away from my face.

I pulled away from her. "Nooooo!" I screamed. "This can't be real!"

My mother started bawling. "I'm so sorry, baby. I didn't know my past would come back to haunt you."

I backed away from her. I turned on my heels and ran away from her, her words, her saying sorry. I kept telling myself that this was a lie, a dream. A fucking nightmare.

But as two COs chased after me and tackled me down to the ground, and as I continued to scream and pinch myself, I never found myself waking up from my bed. I was in the same place, very much awake. I realized this was far from a dream and this was real, very much real, and this was my life . . . My demise.

The End

About the Author

Karen Williams, who also writes as Braya Spice, is the author of *Harlem On Lock, The People vs. Cashmere, Dirty To The Grave, Thug In Me, Sweet Giselle, Aphrodisiacs: Erotic Short Stories*, and *Dear Drama*. She contributed to the anthologies *Around The Way Girls 7* and *Even Sinners Still Have Souls Too*. She graduated from California State University Dominguez Hills with a Bachelor's degree in Literature and Communications. She works as a probation officer and lives in Bellflower, CA with her two kids, Adara, 15, and Bralynn, 3.